ACCUSED

THE CLASSIC HANK JANSON

The first original Hank Janson book appeared in 1946, and the last in 1971. However, the classic era on which we are focusing in the Telos reissue series lasted from 1946 to 1953.

The following is a checklist of those books, which were subdivided into five main series and a number of "specials".

The titles so far reissued by Telos are indicated by way of an asterisk.

Pre-series books

When Dames Get Tough (1946) *
Scarred Faces (1946) *

Series One

1   This Woman Is Death (1948)
2   Lady, Mind That Corpse (1948)
3   Gun Moll For Hire (1948)
4   No Regrets For Clara (1949)
5   Smart Girls Don't Talk (1949)
6   Lilies For My Lovely (1949)
7   Blonde On The Spot (1949)
8   Honey, Take My Gun (1949)
9   Sweetheart, Here's Your Grave (1949)
10 Gunsmoke In Her Eyes (1949)
11 Angel, Shoot To Kill (1949)
12 Slay-Ride For Cutie (1949)

Series Two

13 Sister, Don't Hate Me (1949)
14 Some Look Better Dead (1950) *
15 Sweetie, Hold Me Tight (1950)
16 Torment For Trixie (1950)
17 Don't Dare Me, Sugar (1950)
18 The Lady Has A Scar (1950)
19 The Jane With The Green Eyes (1950)
20 Lola Brought Her Wreath (1950)
21 Lady, Toll The Bell (1950)
22 The Bride Wore Weeds (1950)
23 Don't Mourn Me Toots (1951)
24 This Dame Dies Soon (1951)

Series Three

25 Baby, Don't Dare Squeal (1951)
26 Death Wore A Petticoat (1951)

27 Hotsy, You'll Be Chilled (1951)
28 It's Always Eve That Weeps (1951)
29 Frails Can Be So Tough (1951)
30 Milady Took The Rap (1951)
31 Women Hate Till Death (1951) *
32 Broads Don't Scare Easy (1951)
33 Skirts Bring Me Sorrow (1951) *
34 Sadie Don't Cry Now (1952)
35 The Filly Wore A Rod (1952)
36 Kill Her If You Can (1952)

Series Four

37 Murder (1952)
38 Conflict (1952)
39 Tension (1952)
40 Whiplash (1952)
41 Accused (1952) *
42 Killer (1952)
43 Suspense (1952)
44 Pursuit (1953)
45 Vengeance (1953)
46 Torment (1953) *
47 Amok (1953)
48 Corruption (1953)

Series Five

49 Silken Menace (1953)
50 Nyloned Avenger (1953)

Specials

A   Auctioned (1952)
B   Persian Pride (1952)
C   Desert Fury (1953)
D   Unseen Assassin (1953)
E   One Man In His Time (1953)
F   Deadly Mission (1953)

ACCUSED

by

HANK
JANSON

This edition first published in England in 2004
by Telos Publishing Ltd
61 Elgar Avenue, Tolworth, Surrey, KT5 9JP, England

www.telos.co.uk
Telos Publishing Ltd values feedback.
Please e-mail us with any comments you may have
about this book to: feedback@telos.co.uk

ISBN: 1-903889-86-3
This edition © 2004 Telos Publishing Ltd
Introduction © 2004 Steve Holland

Novel by Stephen D Frances
Cover by Reginald Heade
With thanks to Steve Holland
www.hankjanson.co.uk
Silhouette device by Philip Mendoza
Cover design by David J Howe
This edition prepared for publication by Stephen James Walker
Internal design, typesetting and layout by David Brunt

The Hank Janson name, logo and silhouette device
are trademarks of Telos Publishing Ltd

First published in England by New Fiction Press, October 1952

Printed in India

1 2 3 4 5 6 7 8 9 10 11 12 13 14 15

British Library Cataloguing in Publication Data. A catalogue
record for this book is available from the British Library.

PUBLISHER'S NOTE

The appeal of the Hank Janson books to a modern readership lies not only in the quality of the storytelling, which is as powerfully compelling today as it was when they were first published, but also in the fascinating insight they afford into the attitudes, customs and morals of the 1940s and 1950s. We have therefore endeavoured to make *Accused*, and all our other Hank Janson reissues, as faithful to the original editions as possible. Unlike some other publishers, who when reissuing vintage fiction have been known edit it to remove aspects that might offend present-day sensibilities, we have left the original narrative absolutely intact.

The original editions of these classic Hank Janson titles made quite frequent use of phonetic "Americanisms" such as "kinda", "gotta", "wanna" and so on. Again, we have left these unchanged in the Telos Publishing Ltd reissues, to give readers as genuine as possible a taste of what it was like to read these books when they first came out, even though such devices have since become sorta out of fashion.

The only way in which we have amended the original text has been to correct obvious lapses in spelling, grammar and punctuation – we have, for instance, added question marks in the not-infrequent cases where they were omitted from the ends of questions in the original – and to remedy clear typesetting errors.

Lastly, we should mention that we have made every effort to trace and acquire relevant copyrights in the various elements that make up this book. However, if anyone has any further information that they could provide in this regard, we would be very grateful to receive it.

INTRODUCTION

Accused was one of seven Hank Janson novels found to be obscene fifty years ago at the Old Bailey, and both your publishers and I, your humble host, hasten to point out that in reissuing this work, we do not wish to see our readers depraved or corrupted, nor to contribute to the general slide downwards of literature into an abyss. If you think you might be susceptible to harmful and baleful influences, or feel that the old standards of morals that you have known have slipped away, leaving you and your children a miserable inheritance, this is not the book for you.

If, on the other hand, you want to enjoy a little gem of crime noir, read on.

The Old Bailey obscenity trial involved seven novels, their publisher and their distributor. It was, to put it bluntly, a show trial. The genre of paperback gangster fiction that had sprung up over the previous decade in the wake of such best sellers as *No Orchids For Miss Blandish* and the novels of Peter Cheyney, was on trial. In 1956, a Select Committee formed to investigate the Obscene Publications Bill, then before Parliament, noted that the marked increase in the number of destruction orders issued against books was mainly attributable to the increase in the number of "cheap paper-backed novels dealing with sordid subjects." The Director of Public Prosecutions had, since 1951, compiled a list of books against which destruction orders had been successfully issued. Updated annually and distributed to Chief Constables throughout England and Wales, the list grew dramatically over a period of only three years until it covered hundreds of novels and magazines; a third list compiled by customs officers was later appended. Very few of these books were legally "obscene", since that had to be tested in court before a jury. A destruction order issued by a magistrate could be challenged, but the vast majority of cases involved a handful of books picked up at a local newsagents. The owners, weighing up the cost of a few books against the cost of a court case, invariably let the destruction order

7

proceed, and the books were burned.

Yet the publishing of these "sordid" books continued, and, increasingly, it was the publishers who were put in the dock. Fines ranging from £5 to over £1,000 seemed to be having no impact; as the net widened, books that had been on open sale for years suddenly found themselves added to the DPP's lists, with no indication that they were not recently published. In August 1953, one case against a bookseller involved no fewer than fifteen Hank Janson titles. A few days later, Reginald Carter, Hank's publisher, and Julius Reiter, his distributor, were questioned by Scotland Yard.

The case came to trial at the Old Bailey in January 1954, and was held before the Recorder of London, an ancient and honoured position created in the 13th Century for a permanent full-time advisor to the Lord Mayor and the Court of Aldermen on questions of law. In 1954, the appointee was Gerald Dodson, a man of strong religious convictions and equally strong views formed over a forty-year career at the bar. Dodson chose to hear the trial of seven "obscene libels" ("libels" here meaning, literally, little books) himself, and there can be little doubt that he had formed his opinion of them before a word of evidence was spoken in court. Dodson's response when the defence counsel requested more time for the jury to read all seven of the charged books was to say that an hour and three-quarters was enough. "I have glanced through these books myself, and I am quite well able to form an opinion, with no difficulty at all," he told R C Moore. Gerald Howard QC pointed out that it had taken the prosecuting counsel the same amount of time to read extracts from the books, and Dodson was eventually persuaded to allow the jury more time to read the books as a whole.

Howard and his fellow QC, Christmas Humphreys, knew from past experience of obscenity cases that much of the court's time would be taken up with extracts, and that the litany of stray and out of context paragraphs would blur in the minds of the jury, one image following hot upon another as the prosecution hammered home the point that these were not just "dirty" books but "obscene" books that had the potential to deprave and corrupt readers who were open to such influences.

'FILTHY BOOKS'— PUBLISHERS JAILED

Warrant out for arrest of man who wrote 2s. crime novels

THIS WAS HIS PEN NAME:

ON THE JACKET
The books cost 2s.

By Daily Mail Reporter

A WARRANT has been issued for the arrest of Hank Janson, alleged to be the author of seven obscene books. Such a name could belong to a famous American detective, or to a schoolgirls' comic-strip hero.

HANK JANSON
He is now in Spain.

But Hank Janson is the nom-de-plume of a little man with a small black beard who was summoned in his real name, Stephen Frances, accused of publishing p o r n o graphic literature.

This 40-year-old Englishman is somewhere in Spain. He began his writing career as a serious author of science and detective stories.

From these efforts his rewards were megare; so he became the author of best-seller "dreadfuls."

In three years he wrote 52 books dealing with underworld crime ranging from America to the Arabian Desert.

For the troops

The sales were phenomenal. Every six weeks 100,000 copies of each book were distributed throughout Britain.

Chief among the purchasers of these "works" were Government officials, who, as Mr. Christmas Humphreys, defending counsel, at the Old Bailey yesterday said, were acting on behalf of the three Services.

These books were bought for them by NAAFI officials. They were not "under the counter" books. They could be bought openly at most bookstalls.

Jury read them

Reginald Carter and Julius Reiter—two London publishe s —and three printing compani s were found guilty of publishing seven books which the jury held to be obscene.

The two directors were jailed. The companies were each fined £2,000.

'LITERARY POLLUTION MUST END'

Public drifting to pool of depravity, Recorder warns

TWO men who published obscene books were each jailed for six months at the Old Bailey last night, and their firms were fined a total of £6,000.

Sir Gerald Dodson, Recorder of London, commented : "One can only hope that this trial will mean a sweep towards the realm of pure and exhilarating literature, and not this kind of debasing stuff which, sooner or later, will drag the whole reading public into a veritable pool of depravity."

To jail went 34-year-old Reginald Herbert Carter and Julius Reiter, 46. The A.R.C. Press and the New Fiction Press, of Borough High-street, S.E., and the Gaywood Press, of Gaywood - street, Southwark, were fined

Abyss of filth

The jury spent several hours in their private room reading the books which the prosecution claimed were liable to deprave and corrupt.

The Recorder said to them: "The books must have brought vividly to your minds the abyss of filth to which the nation is drifting."

"It has been said," he went on, "that an obscene publication is to be judged in the light of modern standards. I profoundly disagree, and to the credit of the jury, by their verdict, they showed they entirely disagreed, also.

"The jury are to be complimented in making a stand against this downward tendency. It must have been some consolation to them for their labours, to hear that all these books have been condemned— in some 52 instances all over the country.

Monstrous

"Everybody in this court breathed a little more freely on hearing that. This is literary pollution, and it is high time it came to an end. It is monstrous that anybody should be allowed to make money in that way."

Earlier Mr. Christmas Humphreys—for Reiter and the Gaywood Press—had said that the jury should consider the whole background of sexual publications—what women were allowed to do and say.

"What was on television, in broadcasting, what magazines and books were easily obtainable in shops, and describing things which Hank Janson, author of the books in question, would not dream of publishing."

Dr. Julius Reiter, who was sentenced to six months, is a former German refugee. He found publishing salacious novels was more lucrative than "Westerns." He turned from the cowboy story to the murder of the nude. His turnover jumped from £1,200 a year to £70,000 a year—in ten years.

The warrant for Hank Janson's arrest has been issued for an alleged offence for which he cannot, under extradition treaties, be brought to Britain to face trial.

Daily Mail, January 20, 1954

The defence knew that, of the seven, *Accused* would be the novel on which the case was won or lost and, ahead of the trial, had offered a deal to the prosecution. If the case concentrated on that one novel and it was found to be obscene, they would plead guilty to the other six counts. The deal was rejected.

As predicted, Mervyn Griffith-Jones, the counsel for the prosecution, concentrated heavily on *Accused* when he opened the case, highlighting what he felt were the most obscene passages with a running commentary of events as they unfolded in the novel. To give a brief example, Griffith-Jones quoted:

> I knew we were crazy. But I also knew nothing was going to stop it happening. It was inevitable, something that had to happen, like a car going down hill with no brakes and no means of stopping until it hit bottom.

"It appears in a moment, of course, what is inevitable," added Griffith-Jones. "If you have read all the book up to now, it is perfectly clear that the only thing that is inevitable is the sexual intercourse that is about to take place."

At another point in the case, Griffith-Jones described a scene where "Freidman puts his naked wife over his knees and with a knife is going, apparently, to slit her private parts, and threatens to castrate the young man as soon as he is finished." What Freidman actually says is, "I'm gonna teach you both a lesson you'll never forget." And a few lines later:

> "I'm gonna teach you," he snarled. "I'm gonna learn both of you. You're gonna have a lesson you'll never forget. A permanent reminder you won't be able to stop thinking about the next time you start tom-catting."

No mention of castration, only the vague threat that it would be a "permanent reminder."

Here and elsewhere, Griffith-Jones was bringing his own interpretation to the novel, as all readers do. Stephen

Frances, Hank's creator and author, knew he was writing "hot" stories, but felt that he had never strayed over the line into obscenity. "My stuff was done by innuendo," he told one reporter, many years later. "One minute a man and a woman were sitting side by side. You'd read a whole page and get the impression of physical contact, but you couldn't pin it down." [1]

With this reissue of the much-maligned *Accused*, I hope it will become more obvious to readers that the spin given to the text by Griffith-Jones was an interpretation rather than a straight description. You can find a full transcript of the prosecution evidence, taken from the trial notes, in *The Trials Of Hank Janson*, also available from Telos Publishing Ltd, so it does not need to be repeated here.

Instead, now that we've taken a look at the aftermath, it's interesting to look at the origins of *Accused*. Frances was a prolific writer, churning out sixty-five novels in four and a half years, of which *Accused* was the sixty-third. In March 1952, Reginald Carter began installing a rotary press at his new print works in Friern Barnet and registered the company Arc Press Ltd. At the same time, he took over the defunct Comyns Ltd, and when the new press came on line, launched a slate of new gangster fiction titles. Frances wrote two of the first four titles to get the new series off to a roaring start, *Lovely But Deadly* and *Beauty Found A Grave*, both as Dave Steel. To cope with this sudden increase in his schedule, Frances began working with Geoffrey Pardoe who, two years earlier, had collaborated with Frances on a series of gangster novels for Scion Ltd under the pen name Duke Linton. The working method was for Pardoe to supply a first draft or an extensive synopsis, which Frances would then use as a basis, "slashing and editing" what was already there until he had a story that he dictated in the same way as he dictated the Hank Janson novels at his home in Spain.

And Frances did not limit this working relationship to the Dave Steel byline: Pardoe was also partly responsible for outlining a number of Hank Janson yarns. Following the January 1954 obscenity trial, which resulted in Carter and

---

[1] *Sunday Times*, 25 February 1968.

Jury are locked up to read nine books

Evening
Standard

February
1, 1955

Twelve jurymen filed out of court at the Old Bailey today to begin reading nine books about what the prosecution called "sex and cruelty."

Their task was to decide whether or not the books were obscene and also whether the man who sat in the dock wrote them.

The jury will be locked in their room from 10.30 to 4 p.m. every day—with a break for lunch—until they have "all read all of all the books."

Accused of publishing obscene libels was Stephen Daniel Frances, of Peas Pottage, near Crawley, Sussex, who, the prosecution say, is Hank Janson, author of best-selling paper-back fiction.

He faces seven charges dealing with seven books called Accused, Auction, Persian Pride, Pursuit, Amok, Killer, and Vengeance.

There were not enough copies of the books for each juryman to take home a set so they will have to come to court every day.

Two other books they will have to read are The Jane With The Green Eyes and My Lady Took The Rap.

These two, say the prosecution, Frances admitted writing as Hank Jansen in 1952.

The jury will have to decide whether there is similarity in style and phrasing between these two books and the seven mentioned in the charges.

Sir Anthony Hawke, the Common Serjeant, said he would continue the case tomorrow week.

Frances pleaded not guilty and bail was renewed.

Reiter being sentenced to six months' imprisonment, Frances returned to England to stand trial himself. When the case opened in February 1955, the prosecution hoped to prove, through a comparison of styles, that the seven "obscene" books were by the same author who, during an interview with a Scotland Yard officer, had admitted to writing two earlier titles. Frances pleaded not guilty, and claimed that he had not written a Hank Janson novel since moving to Spain.

The prosecution also tried a second tactic, and obtained payment records from Janson's publisher, New Fiction Press. The company had been driven into liquidation by the £2,000 fine imposed by the Recorder during the earlier trial, and investigators going through the records held by the liquidators discovered cheque stubs made out to Pardoe for various sums, including one for £20 which Pardoe was paid for his outline for *Accused*. The case against Frances consequently collapsed.

12

Whether or not Frances knew that the outline for *Accused* was also a reasonably faithful outline for James M Cain's *The Postman Always Rings Twice* is open to debate. It seems almost impossible to believe that Frances was unaware of Cain's novel, which had originally been published in New York in 1934 and quickly crossed the Atlantic. Jonathan Cape published their first edition in May 1934, and the title had gone through eight impressions by 1942. A year earlier, it had been chosen as the first title to appear under the Guild Books paperback imprint produced by the British Publishers Guild. The movie adaptation, starring Lana Turner and John Garfield, was released in the UK in 1946 with an "A" (for adult) certificate. The book was famous, the film a classic.

Cain's influence on crime fiction was colossal, and, I've always thought, highly influential on the Hank Janson novels. Unlike the traditional hard-boiled stories of Carroll John Daly and Dashiell Hammett, Cain preferred to concentrate on the people who committed crimes, rather than the people who solved them. Where the hard-boiled hero may operate outside the law, he also has his own strict moral codes. Cain's characters have no such codes. They answer only the call of lust and greed. In his two greatest novels, *The Postman Always Rings Twice* and *Double Indemnity*, he also introduces a *femme fatale*, the prize sought by the narrator. Cain's women are as wicked and as manipulative as they are beautiful.

In the majority of the Hank Janson novels, the narrator is none other than Hank himself, and the stories are told through his eyes and emotions. In one sense, this worked to Frances's disadvantage, since Hank, despite his vulnerabilities and flaws, was never allowed to be immoral or weak. He could fall for temptation, but always had to pull back. He could not become a truly tragic figure.

In the novels that didn't feature Janson as a character, this was not the case. There is a tension in these novels above and beyond the regular Janson series, simply because the characters *can* be weak; they *can* give in to their obsessions; and the outcome is never certain. The opening paragraphs of *Accused* will tell you immediately that the ending of the story is going to be anything but happy.

Farran, the narrator, is a weak, tragic character, on the run through unfortunate circumstances. At the diner where he holes up, he has no room of his own, sits at the feet of his master and sleeps on the floor. His life is dominated by Freidman, although Friedman himself is not physically commanding and described as "maybe forty-five, running to fat, with grey hairs freely sprinkling the sides of his temples ... his arms were thick and fleshy, his skin white and clammy." Yet Farran's misfortune puts Freidman in a position of power, which he exploits mercilessly and sadistically.

In this, Farran shares a bond with Freidman's wife, because she, too, is trapped in her own circle of hell in the diner's kitchen: "The coffee and soup were simmering, sending drifting vapour clouds up towards the ceiling. The sun was beating down on the iron roof, baking the air inside, turning it into an unbearable inferno." Freidman's wife suffers the torments of the damned, both in the kitchen and in the bedroom. Frances further dehumanises her by the simple but effective device of never naming her.

The plot of *Accused* unfolds quickly and is told in heat-soaked flashbacks intercut with snatches from the grim, uncompromising present, as if the book was edited for MTV. Obsession and passion and tragedy are played out in the bleached white of a desert, and escaping the burning sun only leads to another circle of hell.

Of the 253 original novels that appeared under the Hank Janson byline, this is one of the best. Because it was judged to be obscene, it has not been in print for over fifty years, so it gives me particular pleasure to say:

Welcome to Henry Farran's nightmare.

Steve Holland
Colchester, February 2004

CHAPTER ONE

It was a heavy iron door, and it clanged echoingly as it swung open. Their shadows, thrown against the wall by the dim light, loomed immense, cautious and watchful.

There were three of them: two in uniform, and a third man I hadn't seen before. He was heavily built, merging into fatness, and the fleshiness of his face beneath the grey fedora was emphasised by the heavy shadows thrown by that single, dim roof light.

Apprehensively, I swung my feet off the bunk, slid along it until my shoulders pressed against the wall. That was as far as I could get from them.

The fat guy stared at me for a long while, said nothing. The two uniformed guys stood shoulder to shoulder behind him, watched expressionlessly.

I felt sick inside, instinctively raised my hands to protect my face, and the clink of the steel chain that linked my hands together made me feel even sicker.

That fat guy kept on staring at me. It was like he was trying to beat me with his eyes. And as he stared, he fumbled in his pocket for a toothpick, carefully gouged a fragment of food from between his back teeth, spat it out thoughtfully.

He spat it at me. I felt it on my forehead, and it was like the brand of red hot iron. But I was learning sense. I lifted my hands to my bruised face, wiped my sleeve across my forehead, suppressed the spark of hopeless anger inside me.

"You're coming with us, Farran," he said, and his voice was soft and oily.

I felt faint, felt the chill sweat trickling between my shoulders. "Where?" I croaked. "Where are we going?"

"You know where," he growled smoothly. "But today you've got *me* for company."

I didn't want it to happen again, but I couldn't stop it. The whimper kinda leaked out of my mouth from deep down inside me. "No." I pleaded. "Not again. Not again!"

He chuckled. A long, low chuckle that went on like it was never gonna stop. It was evil, malicious and threatening, completely devoid of humour.

"All right, let's go," he said.

I cringed away from him until the hard, cold brick-work was hurting my shoulders. "No," I whimpered. "Not again. Not again."

"There's two ways of coming," he said, smiling gently like he was getting ready to enjoy himself. "Which way is it gonna be?"

The sheer hopelessness of everything washed over me. There was no escape. Every nerve in my body shrieked a protest at going with them. But to resist would be worse.

He made a slight gesture, and the two uniformed figures behind him began to move towards me. I knew what they would do, and almost before I knew it, I was on my feet, whimpering again. "No. No. No! Don't touch me. I'm coming."

The big guy chuckled again, that same, slow, evil chuckle. He stepped to one side, motioned to me to go out ahead of him.

My knees were like chalk, crumbling and uncertain. And as I took shaky, uncertain paces, the clink of chains and the chaffing soreness of my wrists and ankles hammered in at me again the hopelessness of everything, the impossibility of escape, the grim finality of it all.

The two uniformed figures closed in on me, each taking an arm, fingers strong and corded, biting deep into my arms. Their shadowed faces were emotionless, but I could sense the smouldering, bitter hatred inside them, the hate that was seeking an excuse to exert itself. I sweated with fear, my feet dragging and my hands trembling.

It wasn't far to go, and I knew the way. I'd been there a coupla times before. One of them opened the door and they half-dragged, half-pushed me inside.

It was the same, airless, windowless, white-washed stone room. The same small wooden table and wooden chairs scattered around the room. One of them dragged a heavy wooden chair into the middle of the room, motioned me to climb upon my throne of torture.

16

I shuffled over to it, the chains between my ankles and wrists clinking mockingly. And there was hopeless dread inside me, a bitter, anguished fear of the inevitable. There was nothing but suffering and suffering. My shoulders drooped, my head hung heavy, the chains were an enormous weight that weighed down my limbs. I sat there, dull and hopeless, waiting while one of the guards closed the door and the other switched on the light above my head.

I was expecting it. But even so, it hit me with the impact of a flame thrower. A white, heatless light smashing down at me with brutalising force, making my muscles knot and jump, re-creating in a split second all the atmosphere of pain, terror and panic that was associated with that white glare.

They waited in the shadows beyond the halo thrown by that powerful, torturing light, watched my body jerking and twitching, and gauged the terror and apprehension I was undergoing. They waited until my jangling nerves had partially soothed, until the jerking of my muscles had become mere twitches.

Then, moving quietly and silently like a slithering snake, the fat guy moved around back of me.

I tensed, felt my muscles knot, closed my eyes and waited in numbed apprehension.

He came up behind me, so close I could feel his breath hot on the back of my neck. He said, in a voice that throbbed with hatred: "You've got *me* to look after you today."

I remained tight-lipped, tried to relax so the pain would wash over me, carrying away the numbed and agonised tyrant that my mind would become.

"You sonofabitch," he said quietly, and he spat out the words with a quiet venom that terrified me, although I had become accustomed to the hatred in the words and eyes of these men.

"You goddam sonofabitch," he snarled.

I took a deep breath, tried to slump and relax my nerves.

His fingers bit deep into the back of my neck like steel forceps, holding, gouging and twisting nerve centres, turning my body rigid, shoulders hunched and my lungs motionless.

17

"You swine," he snarled, and the fingers gouged deeper, like he wanted to tear out my nerve centres by the roots. Under the sharp, almost unbearable agony of it, I tried to drag away from him.

His other hand was ready, fingers sliding across my scalp, grasping hair with steel fingers so my head was held immovable, the piercing, shrieking pain gouging ever deeper into my neck and brain.

I did it without thinking, used my chained hands to fight myself free from the nauseating agony. And immediately a savage jerk dragged me sideways off balance, so that I crashed to the stone floor with the chair on top of me.

He stood over me, looming immense, a huge bulk blocking out part of the glaring light, his fingers crooked in uncontrollable anger.

"You still wanna kill, damn you?" he snarled. "You still wanna kill, huh?"

I knew what was coming, tensed myself and closed my eyes. When the toe of his boot drove into my side, it was pain, but an old pain, a familiar pain. It was as though I had no ribs. There was just a hole, and the toe-cap penetrated inside me through the open, tender wound.

"All right. Climb back on that chair."

That was the subtlety of it. Again and again climbing back on to the chair. It was like being led again and again to the place of torture.

I stumbled to my feet awkwardly, the inevitable chains clinking between my ankles and wrists. I fumbled awkwardly with the chair, because of that hole in my side. It caused me to bend over sideways like I was deformed.

"On the chair," he snarled.

I slumped on the chair, heard my lungs rasping, the breath making a hoarse sound in my throat.

He was there behind me, his fingers resting gently on my shoulders. His gentle touch made me shudder afresh.

"What's your name?" he demanded.

I licked my lips, said nothing. What was the use? Everything was hopeless.

His strong fingers came over my shoulders, down around my neck, gripping the lapels of my jacket so he could draw it back, pull the jacket down over my shoulders, half-imprisoning my upper arms.

"What's your name?" he asked again, softly and menacingly.

I still said nothing.

His arms were around front of me, undid the buttons of my shirt, dragged my shirt down over my shoulders. I could feel my skin pricking like it was over-sensitised, and I moaned like the arc-light beating down on my flesh was a searing ray.

"I'm asking you for the third time," he said softly. "What's your name?"

It wouldn't make any difference if I told him. It would happen just the same. I just hung my head and waited.

There was no way of knowing what it would be, and there was no sound to warn me. I was so beaten, so shocked by the nightmare of the last forty-eight hours, that I hadn't even the nerve to look over my shoulder.

Yet even though I was expecting it, when it did come, the sheer, blinding, shocking agony of it made me convulse, throw myself bodily off the chair, writhe and scream and greet the insanity of agony nibbling like some fiery demon at the outer edges of my mind.

They let me lie there until my pain-drenched body ceased twitching and quivering. I pushed myself up into a sitting position, the sweat running down my forehead, trickling down into my eyes, causing them to smart. But the seat of the pain was in my shoulder, a white hot needle burning through flesh and muscle. My lips were quirking as I lifted my heavy head, peered up at the heavy bulk overshadowing me, searched for the means by which he could inflict such shocking agony with such ease.

I should have known it would have been something subtle. Something that would show no scars, something that inflicted great suffering without visible effects.

It was a glistening, two inch needle, slender and evilly pointed, spliced into a wooden haft. I'd been stabbed with it, greedy metal biting into my shoulder, skewering flesh and metal, twisting and torturing nerves and sinew but showing only the merest pinpoint of blood instead of the tell-tale marks of unlawful torture.

He said softly, like it was an invitation to make myself at home: "Get up. Sit on the chair."

I couldn't face it again. I'd been writhing for two or three minutes in a mist of agony. I just couldn't make myself get to my feet and sit on the chair, my quivering flesh yet awaiting another stab.

He moved in quietly, swung his foot. His toe-cap smashed through the hole in my side, sent fiery trailers scorching through my body.

"Get up," he snarled.

I wanted to be sick. I just couldn't go on taking it. No human being could go on taking it. The next time, his toe-cap seemed to penetrate into my stomach, exploded there, sending sparks of white hot pain shooting through my body to the tips of the extremities.

"On your feet," he said again, just as quietly, and this time it wasn't necessary, because I was already on my knees, my body twisted, doubled, yet blindly clambering to its feet, reaching for the chair.

He whispered: "You aren't very smart at answering questions, are you?"

I breathed hard, wished I could faint before they killed me. This was more than human flesh and blood could stand.

"The name's Farran, isn't it," he said.

"Yeah," I grunted.

"Henry Warren Farran?"

"Yeah," I breathed.

He was around in front of me, right up close, thrusting his heavy, greasy face towards me. There was murderous hatred in his black eyes. "A killer," he snarled. "Kill like a mad dog. You're a killer, Farran. A mad killer."

"I'm not," I panted desperately. "That's what everyone says, but it s not true. I'm not ...."

He stabbed again, this time stabbing down at my thigh so hard that the wooden haft bruised my flesh through my trousers and the needle skewered muscle and flesh like a jagged shaft of glass gouging deep into my leg.

20

They left me for ten minutes to recover from that. The fat guy smoked a cigarette, watched me all the time, like he was calculating just how much more I could take.

I was exhausted, the strength drawn out of me so I was weak like a sick child.

He tossed away the butt end of his cigarette, crossed over to me, grasped a handful of my hair and jerked my bead up, dragged me to my feet.

"You're Farran, aren't you?" he demanded again.

I was so weak the words could barely escape my lips. "Yeah."

"You're a crazy killer!"

I licked my lips, said nothing.

"Why d'ya kill Freidman?" he stormed suddenly. "A regular guy who gave you a job, looked after you, treated you swell. Why d'you kill him!"

"He ... I ..."

"For a few hundred bucks," he snarled explosively. "For a few lousy, measly bucks, you bumped off the guy that befriended you."

"You don't understand," I panted. "You don't understand the way ...."

"Sure," he rasped. "I understand. Just the way you're gonna understand. This is where you start in understanding."

I wasn't prepared for it. Even if I had been, I couldn't have done anything about it. His fingers were still locked in my hair as he swung his fist, swung it with all his strength, against the side of my jaw, slapping me off my feet, spinning sideways, splaying on the floor with my head, mind and the room, all revolving together in a loud, rushing noise.

At the end of the long, roaring tunnel, his words came rolling down towards me, threatening and filtering through a blur of blinding light.

"Freidman," said the rolling voice.

"Freidman," the voice echoed, long and down, down into the depths of my mind and soul.

"Mad killer!"

"Freidman."

"Freidman."

"Freidman!"

21

CHAPTER TWO

I climbed aboard the truck when it stopped to re-fuel. I was quick and the driver didn't see me. He stopped twice after that to eat, and I didn't dare move, because I didn't want him to throw me off.

But luck was dead against me. Because, maybe an hour after the last stop, I fell asleep, and a pot-hole the truck bumped over, caught me unawares, catapulted me out from beneath the cover of a tarpaulin, rolled me over among the crates.

Yeah, luck was against me. Because the driver looked behind to make sure everything was all right and saw me.

He jammed on his brakes.

I'd already been caught once by a truck driver. I was over the tailboard and sprinting back along the road by the time he climbed down out of his cabin.

He stood looking at me, hands on his hips, scowling balefully.

I watched him apprehensively from a distance, ready to start running if necessary.

He walked slowly around back of the truck, climbed up over the tailboard, checked to make sure I hadn't damaged any of the goods he was carrying. Then he turned around, stared at me, shook his fist.

I watched him warily.

He said angrily, "I could get sacked for having you ride back here."

I kept my distance, said nothing.

"You can start walking now, you sonofabitch," he snarled. "It's miles to the next town. I hope you enjoy it."

He jumped down over the tailboard, walked around to the driver's cabin, watching me all the time. He was worried I was gonna try boarding the truck again.

I wasn't gonna risk it. He was broad-shouldered, with hands like hams. He could smash my jaw with one slam. He watched me through the driving mirror as he started the engine, got the truck rolling, and there wasn't anything I could do except stand in the middle of the road and watch him slowly pull away from me.

I watched until all that was left of him was a puff of dust on the road ahead. Then I sat at the side of the road and took off my boots.

It was hot, the sun beating down with a heat that could boil my brains in my skull. Up till now I'd been protected by the tarpaulin. Now I was out from the shade, it was like I using roasted.

I looked around hopelessly. The narrow ribbon of dusty road stretched in front and behind as far as the eye could see, flanked either side by sandy scrubland that shimmered in the heat. The scrub was dried up and brittle in the hot air that clogged and choked like invisible cotton wool.

I tied the laces of my boots together, stripped off my jacket, slung them across my shoulders and started walking.

The dusty road was hot, burning. But walking bare-footed was more comfortable than having my swollen feet chafed by hard leather.

I kept walking, kept following the road.

It had been a lousy break. This was just about the worst possible place to be ditched. That truck driver hadn't been joking. The last town we'd passed had been at least thirty miles behind us. This was a second-class road, and the chances of being given a lift were few. It looked like I was going to have an uncomfortable twenty-four hours ahead of me before reaching the next town.

The sun beat down remorselessly.

I kept on walking, walking, walking.

I was sweating, the sun beating down and my mouth parched; my nostrils clogged with the dust kicked up by my sore feet.

I don't know how long I'd been walking when I saw it in the distance. Probably I'd been walking for hours. It was not much more than a shack at the side of the road with a sun porch built at the front.

Maybe a coupla hundred yards before I reached it, I saw the weather-beaten, sun-dried sign that read: "Snacks."

I kept on walking, came up level with the shack.

It looked deserted, desolate. The dried earth in front of the veranda was caked hard where cars and trucks had pulled in. And it was a real dump. The kinda place no-one would stop if there was an alternative. And I hadn't seen any competition around.

A sign hung over the porch. It read: *A. Freidman – Snacks.*

My nostrils were clogged with dust, my tongue dry like a piece of leather, and my throat lined with sand paper. I dug down in my trouser pockets, counted my money. I had seventy-five cents.

It was getting dark now. And I'd heard that the night can be paralysingly cold in the open country after the heat of the day.

Hobbling painfully now, I crossed to the veranda steps, climbed them slowly, crossed the sun porch, hesitated a moment with my hand on the wire-gauze door before, with sudden resolution, I thrust at it, pushed inside.

It wasn't much more than a normal-sized room with chairs and tables scattered around. A counter ran along the back of the room and two doors led off from behind the counter, one on the left and one on the extreme right. As I opened the door, a bell jangled alarmingly, and almost at once a door on the right opened. A burly, big-built man, sweating visibly through his grimy, collarless shirt, stared at me sullenly. "Just in time", he grunted. "We're just gonna close up; we shut at sundown."

"I won't keep you more than a minute," I said, desperately anxious not to be a nuisance.

"That's okay," he grunted, wiping his hands on his damp shirt. "What d'ya want?"

I gulped, felt the dust coating my throat. "A glass of water," I said.

He stopped wiping his hands on his shirt, stared at me like he thought I was crazy. I became acutely conscious of my dishevelled hair, my unwashed face, the dusty boots slung over my shoulders and my grimy shirt that hadn't been washed in days.

He said abruptly: "How d'ya get here, kid? This is fifty miles from anywhere."

I took a deep breath. "Walked."

"Walked!"

"Fella gave me a lift part of the way," I mumbled. "I decided I'd walk a bit for exercise."

He was grinning now; grinning at my stupidity. Grinning because I thought he would believe me.

"Thirsty, huh?" he said.

"Yeah!"

He didn't say anything, turned on his heel, disappeared into the room behind him. It was probably the kitchen. A few moments later, he came out with a glass of water, slid it across the counter towards me.

I sipped it slowly, wanting to savour it, relish every last drop of it, enjoy the cleansing feeling as it sluiced down my throat, cool and fresh, washing away the hot, gritty dust that was choking me. And while I drank, he was giving me the once-over with a kind of mocking, knowing grin.

I gave him the once-over too, judged him to be maybe forty-five, running to fat, with grey hairs freely sprinkling the sides of his temples, and bushy black eyebrows that cast his deep-set brown eyes into shadow. He had a long nose that was hard and cruel and matched his hard, cruel lips that were now twisted in a malicious sneer.

His arms were thick and fleshy, his skin white and clammy, and his grimy, sweaty shirt gaped open down to his navel. His shirt was heavy with the smell of sweat and his face was damp and shiny, glistening with fresh perspiration a few seconds after he wiped the back of his arm across his forehead.

I set down the empty glass, breathed a sigh of relief.

"Want another?" he asked.

"Yeah," I grunted. "Sure could go it."

He took my glass, disappeared inside. When he came back and set down the glass in front of me, I saw that his fat, sausage-like fingers were soft and white, looked almost obscene with the thick black hairs that sprouted from the backs of his fingers.

"Going far?" he asked, slyly.

25

"Yeah, travelling across State," I said, offhandedly.

There was silence while I sipped the water.

"Where you heading?"

Beyond knowing I was somewhere in Arizona, I hadn't the faintest idea where I was, or where I was going. "The next town along," I said.

He nodded as though he understood exactly what I had in my mind.

"What's your name, kid?" he asked.

Some of the water went down the wrong way. I coughed, spluttered. When I was through coughing he was grinning at me. "What's your name, kid?" he asked again.

"Brown," I said. "John Brown."

"A mighty nice name," he said, mockingly.

"Yeah."

Nothing more was said until I put down the glass. I took a firmer grip on my jacket, squared my shoulders, said briskly: "Thanks for everything, mister. Much obliged."

I'd at first thought it might be possible to spend the night there.

Now I'd decided I'd prefer to spend the night on the road.

He said, smoothly: "That'll be a dollar, kid."

I stared at him. "What are you talking about?"

"Two glasses of water. That'll cost you a dollar."

I turned on my heel abruptly, walked towards the door.

For a man his size, he could move with amazing speed. I didn't realise that until it was too late, until he was standing with his back to the door, between me and freedom.

"Not so fast, kid," he said. He was still grinning, but there was sly cunning in his eyes.

"Water don't cost anything," I said. "Everyone knows that."

"It costs here," he said. "This is twenny miles from anywhere. Good money had to be spent for that well to be dug. Water has to be drawn from that well, kept on ice. That's worth dough in anybody's language."

I flushed angrily. He was twice as broad as me, more than a head taller. His brawny, fleshy arms could crush me in a bear-like embrace. I said, with a choke in my voice: "I haven't even got a dollar. I'm broke."

26

He nodded approvingly. "Yeah, that's what I figured."

"I'd pay you if I had the dough," I said.

"Don't worry, kid," he smiled, genially. "We'll even it up. I'll put a call through to Claremont. I'll ask the cops to look in."

For a long time it was like the world stood still. I hadn't eaten all day, and maybe that made me feel faint. I knew that all the colour had drained from my face.

He said softly, suavely: "It's like I figured, kid. You're scared of the cops, aren't you?"

"No," I said quickly, scared. "They ain't got nothing on me."

"You ain't got nothing to worry about then, kid." He grinned. "I'll just give them a call. Maybe they'll even give you a lift into Claremont."

My hand was shaking. I tried to stop it from shaking as I drew my seventy-five cents from my pocket, thrust it at him. "This is all I've got," I pleaded. "It ought to be enough. Take it, will you?"

He shook his head slowly, grinned expansively, reached out a huge hand that enveloped my shoulder, twisted me around and gave me a shove towards the counter.

"Sit down, kid," he invited.

I watched him apprehensively as I climbed up on one of the rickety, four-legged high stools.

He stood staring at me for a long time. He said, softly: "You're in trouble, kid. Where d'you aim to spend tonight? How far d'you think seventy-five cents is gonna take you? I don't know what you've done, but what makes you think the cops won't pick you up when you get to Claremont?"

He was repeating all the arguments I'd been telling myself over and over again for the last few hours. I let my head fall and my shoulders droop.

He went on talking, softly, smoothly. "It sticks out like a sore thumb, kid. You're on the run from the cops. I can see it a mile off. Every time you pass a cop, he's gonna pick you up on suspicion. You've got that kinda look about you. What do you figure you're gonna do? Where do you figure you're gonna hide out?"

27

I buried my face in my hands, tried to stop my shoulders from shaking, tried to stop the sobs welling up from deep down inside me.

"How old are you, kid?" he said kindly.

"Twenty," I told him.

"Just a kid," he said sympathetically. "What about your family?"

I shook my head, soundlessly.

"All right, kid," he said gently. "Come clean. What did you do? Tell me. Maybe I can help you."

I shook my head, anguish crushing my heart. "Nothing," I gritted. "I didn't do anything."

There was a long pause. He said quietly: "I could help you."

It was a long while before the full meaning of his words hit me. I looked up at him slowly, found his brown eyes watching me calculatingly, saw his cruel lips twist into a cynical grin.

"You wanna place to hide up for a while, don't you, kid? You wanna job, don't you? You want something to eat, and somewhere to sleep. Ain't that right, kid?"

I nodded dumbly, wonderingly.

"Maybe it's better you don't tell me anything," he went on. "What I don't know, I don't have to worry about. Then maybe after a coupla months, you can get on the move again. When things have blown over."

I stared at him.

He nodded at me. "Sure," he said. "I'll give you a break. Trade's brisk this time of the year in the mornings. I can do with help. I'll make you a deal. I'll give you food, a roof to sleep under and no questions asked. What do you say?"

I went on staring at him.

"What the hell's the matter with you?" he demanded. "Are you dumb or something?"

"You mean ..." I faltered. "You mean ... a job here ...with you!"

"And no questions asked," he finished.

I couldn't believe my ears. It was too good to be true. It was like having my wildest dreams answered. But I still wasn't gonna admit to anything. "I haven't done anything," I said in

28

a whisper. "Sure, I wanna job. But I haven't done anything. The cops are not after me."

"No questions asked," he grunted. "D'you want the job or don't you?"

"Sure," I said, eagerly. "I told you. I'm broke. I want a job bad."

"You've got a job," he said.

I looked around the joint. It was dusk now, the sun setting rapidly. "What do I do?"

"It's like I said," he told me. "There's a good, brisk morning trade here. Truck drivers who've been travelling overnight, car salesmen on their way north. I open at six, keep going right through the day till late afternoon. That's when things get quiet."

He jerked his head towards the door. "Quiet like it is now."

"What do I do?"

He gestured. "Clean the place up, keep it swept and cleaned, carry the cups and plates to the tables, watch the customers, make sure they don't leave without paying, draw water from the well, various other odd jobs about the joint that need doing."

"And I can stop here at night?" I asked breathlessly.

'That's in the deal."

I breathed a deep sigh. "I guess that's mighty kind of you, Mr ... Mr Freidman."

His brown eyes were suddenly hard and calculating. "You know my name, huh?"

"Yeah. Saw it painted over the door."

"Well, from now on, it's Sir. D'you get that? You call me Sir. Understand?"

"Yes, Sir," I said, meekly.

Freidman.
FREIDMAN.
FREIDMAN!
The rolling words came swooping down at me, caught me up, lifted me high, shook me, and I felt warm, salty liquid bubbling into my mouth.

"Farran," said a harsh, compelling voice.

There was something about that name. Something that was important. I tried to hold on to the thought, but the rushing in my ears and the numbness of my face was defeating me.

"Farran!"

The name beat at my eardrums, beat at my brain, smashed at my subconsciousness so I knew I had to respond, could not allow myself to drown in the pained mist that was enveloping me.

"Farran," crackled the voice, and a thousand pinpoints of liquid fire were stabbing my head, tearing and rending, the sharpness of the pain driving away the mist. I opened my eyes with an effort, blinked in the glaring white heat of the arc-lamp, tried to get my feet underneath me so that the pain of being hoisted aloft by my hair would be eased. Rocked in a sea of numbed agony, I turned my eyes upward, appealingly.

He was between the light and me now, his shadowy, fleshy face close to mine.

"A crazy, damned killer," he snarled. "Just a mad dog. Just a mad dog running amok." I saw his lips purse and felt his spittle trickle down my forehead.

"Just a mad dog" he snarled. "A decent, hard-working guy, gives you a break and you kill him. Kill him for a few measly bucks. Kill him ruthlessly and mercilessly."

" You don't ... understand ...," I tried to say. But the words wouldn't come out, because of my puffed and bleeding lips.

"This guy, Freidman," he snarled. "He was like a father to you. But you butchered him, murdered him for his dough."

"I ..."

I didn't see his swinging fist, only sensed it. It made a meaty sound as it smashed against my jaw. But I didn't even feel the pain. The force of the blow lifted me off my feet, and it seemed like I was drifting on a cloud. When I smashed against the stone wall moments later, it was a shock and unexpected.

I knew I was slumped there on the stone floor, my head against the hard brick wall and blood pumping from my nostrils. Black waves of pain and faintness were washing ever and ever higher over me, and I wanted to be sick.

Nothing was real.

30

Nothing existed.

I was alone in a drifting world of hardness that had no substance. And that long tunnel of light was searching down towards me, revolving around and around the harsh voice that rasped again and again:

"Freidman!"

"Freidman!"

"Freidman!"

CHAPTER THREE

It was almost dark now. Freidman switched on the lights, crossed to a corner of the room where there was a soft broom. "You can start in, now," he grunted. "Get the place cleaned up. I want everything clean and fresh for the morning."

I was only too willing. But I hadn't eaten all day. I said, flushing shamefacedly: "I can work better with something under my belt."

He stared at me like I'd tried to insult him. Then he said, not unkindly: "Get the place cleaned up first, kid. We'll talk about eating afterwards."

I swept the place thoroughly, pushed all the chairs and tables to one side of the room so I could do it. He sat in one of the chairs, smoking, watching me unblinkingly.

When I was through, I looked at him, expectantly.

He said: "It needs a wash-down as well." He jerked his head at me to indicate I was to follow, hoisted himself from his chair with an effort, led the way around the other side of the counter.

I followed him, was right on his heels when he went through into the back room. As I had guessed, it was the kitchen. But I got a surprise, too.

Because I'd figured Freidman lived there alone.

He didn't. There was a dame in the kitchen. She'd been there all the time and had made just about as much noise as a mouse.

Without any introduction or explanation, he said: "Show the boy how to draw water from the well. He'll do it in the future."

She nodded, held her head low, like she was afraid to look either him or me in the face. She went over to a long, trough-like sink, bent down, fished out three tin buckets, straightened up, holding two buckets in one hand and one in the other hand.

32

Freidman said, quietly: "Let the boy do it. It's his job from now on."

Wordlessly, she passed me the buckets. She still didn't look at me. It was like she was afraid, frightened to do or say the wrong things.

There was a back door to the kitchen. She opened it, led the way through, me following behind her. It wasn't far to the well. Maybe ten or fifteen yards, and in the light streaming through the open kitchen door and cutting through the blackness, we had all the light we needed.

It was a primitive type of well, not much wider than a man's body, surrounded by a low parapet and operated by a hand-winch.

With a practised but weary movement, she attached the bucket to the end of the coarse rope, allowed it to go plummeting down into the blackness of the well, controlling the speed of its descent by the rope running through her fingers.

I watched her as she did it, found it was difficult to stop watching her. She was young, maybe twenty-three or twenty-four. Her hair was rich, black, wavy, and at that moment, damp with sweat. She had brown eyes that wouldn't meet mine, soft, oval features, bright red lips that were just the tiniest bit too ripe and pronounced, and a skin that was naturally brown.

She was dressed simply – very simply! It was a faded black dress, short-sleeved with a discreet vee of a neck-line in and tied at the waist by a belt that gave shape to the dress. The skirt was pleated and reached to just below her knees. She was barefooted, and her legs and feet were brown, kinda healthy-looking.

Even now, it was still hot in that kitchen. During the heat of the afternoon, it musta been an oven. And she hadn't had time to cool off. Her face was shiny and damp, sweat patches blotched her armpits, and her youthful breasts seemed weary, sagged heavily against the damp bodice of the worn dress.

The bucket hit water far down, and she shook the rope, making sure the bucket would overturn, sink and be filled with water. I was wondering why she worked at a dump like this, wondering where she lived, when I saw the wedding ring on her finger.

The significance of it was too obvious to miss. But I just couldn't believe it. This young dame! Married to a guy like Freidman!

I just couldn't believe it.

She reached for the winch-handle, began to turn it.

Freidman's voice said from the doorway: "It's the boy's job. Let him do it."

I flushed, took the winch-handle and began to wind up the bucket. Now I wouldn't look at her any more, in the same way she wouldn't look at me. I had the uncomfortable feeling that Freidman was watching me every moment, watching my face and reading my thoughts as I gave the dame the once-over.

She waited quietly until I'd drawn all three buckets of water. Then she picked up one bucket and led the way inside the kitchen, leaving me to carry the other two buckets.

Freidman stood to one side as we passed through the door, and I felt his eyes resting on me, probing and analysing. I felt a flush spread up from my neck to my cheeks.

"Getting water's one of your most important jobs, boy," he said. "Any time water's wanted for any reason, you get it. Understand?"

"Okay," I said.

"What's that?" he snarled.

"Yes, Sir," I said meekly.

He grunted. "That's better."

He said to the dame: "You got the soup ready for the morning?"

"Yes, Arthur," she said meekly. She had a low, husky voice and spoke like she wasn't used to talking.

"Stove all ready to light up?"

She nodded dumbly towards the stove. He went over to it, gravely inspected the big boiler that was half-full of cold soup. There was another boiler filled with coffee. He glanced around the kitchen with an approving eye. It was as clean as it could possibly be, every metal object shining brightly, everything that could be washed on hand and ready for use in the morning. There was a mountain of soup dishes, cups

34

and plates neatly stacked, which gave an idea of the business they did of a morning.

"Okay, son," he ordered. "You can scrub out the dining room now. Draw more water to replace what you use."

I went down on my hands and knees, scrubbed out the dining room thoroughly. When I was through, I was sweating, my shirt sticking to me. And it felt like my stomach was sticking to my back bone. I was as hungry as a horse.

Just after I'd started scrubbing, Freidman had come out from the kitchen, taken a chair and had watched me with unwavering, unblinking eyes. When I was through, I looked up at him expectantly.

"Hungry, huh?"

I nodded. "I sure am."

I caught the warning glint in his eyes, corrected myself hurriedly. "Yes, sir!"

He levered himself out of his chair, jerked his head as an instruction to follow him.

The dame was still in the kitchen, hunched over the sink, washing table napkins and tea cloths.

"Get the boy something to eat," he instructed.

She straightened up in a way that showed her back ached intolerably, drew her forearm across her forehead, dried her hands on a towel.

She crossed to a big cupboard, opened it up, dug out a jar of pickled onions, a half loaf of bread, a dish of butter, a large ham and a slab of cheese.

She put a clean plate on the table, took a knife and fork from a drawer and then wearily went back to the sink, continued scrubbing.

Freidman was watching her and watching me with a kinda cunning interest. He said, "Take what you want, boy. Help yourself."

That was when I discovered there wasn't a chair in the kitchen. Not one chair! It looked like the dame didn't get a chance to sit down all day.

He said: "Go right ahead. Just help yourself." From the way he said it, I knew it was gonna be this way all time, just cutting myself a hunk of bread and a slice of ham, living on snacks all the time.

"Give the boy a glass of milk," he said.

Once again, she straightened up wearily, got a glass, filled it with milk that was slightly sour, unpleasantly warm.

All the time I was eating, he was watching me, making me uncomfortable, making me feel I was a pawn in some monstrous game that he was playing.

When I was through, I gathered up the ham, carried it towards the cupboard.

He said sharply: "Stop that."

I looked at him in surprise.

"It's her job," he snarled. "All the work in the kitchen is her job. You don't do anything in the kitchen. All you do is draw water. Understand?"

There was anger in his voice. I gulped, said, "Yes, sir," and put the ham back on the table.

"Clear the table," he rapped.

I stood there and watched her do it, uncomfortable because I had to stay there and watch. The dame looked worn out.

"All right, boy," he said, when she was through. "Let's go."

He led the way back into the dining room. He'd already switched on the sign that announced the cafe was closed. He pointed to a chair. "Sit there," he ordered, and as I obediently sat down, he settled himself in another chair, began reading a news-sheet a customer had left behind.

I sat there for almost half an hour, fidgety, with nothing to do. Twice he glanced up at me and the third time he said in a warning voice: "Ain't you happy here, son?"

It was the red light. Even though he hadn't said it, I knew he was thinking of the cops.

"Sure ... yes, Sir," I said hurriedly.

"Sit quietly, then," he said.

It was maybe an hour later when she came through from the kitchen. She moved silently on bare feet, as though afraid of waking a slumbering giant. Freidman glanced up, watched her with cold eyes as she quietly took a chair a few feet away from us, sank into it with obvious relief but a strained look on her face.

Freidman's eyes went back to the newspaper.

36

I watched the girl.

She still wouldn't look at me. Her eyes were lowered like she was afraid to look anyone in the face. And now, underneath the sharp light of the dining room, I could see how tired she was, see the black rings under her eyes and the effort it needed to keep her head erect. Her back musta been aching, too, because she moved cautiously in the chair like it gave her pain to move.

We sat there for maybe another half-an-hour, the only noise being the rustle of the newspaper as Freidman turned the pages. Then he yawned, stretched his arms, dug down in his trouser pocket and came up with a watch, which he inspected carefully.

He got up slowly, stretched once again, moved over to the second door, the room I hadn't yet seen.

Obediently, silently, with eyes lowered, she got to her feet, followed him across to the door, stood waiting meekly with hands at her sides, while he dug down in his pocket for a Yale key. When he opened up, the girl pushed through inside the room. Freidman didn't quite close the door behind her. He paused with his hand on the doorknob, looked at me steadily. "Get some sleep, son," he ordered. "I want you up at five o'clock to help take in the bread when the baker calls. The milk comes about ten minutes after. Understand?"

"Yes, Sir," I gulped.

"And I don't want the lights left on. Understand? Turn them off now."

"Yes, Sir."

"Well. Turn them off!"

I gulped. "Where do I sleep?"

His eyes widened with surprise. Then his lips twisted in that cruel grin of his. "What's the matter with the floor, son?"

"Yes, Sir," I said meekly.

"Turn off the lights, then," he ordered. "All except the 'Closed' sign."

He waited while I turned off the lights. A thin slither of light penetrated from his bedroom. His huge bulk blocked my vision as he passed inside, closed and bolted the door behind him.

It was a strange set-up. Freidman was a strange guy. I couldn't understand him. I was sure he had some special motive in giving me a job. But for the life of me, I couldn't see what it was.

I shucked off my jacket, folded it to form a pillow, stretched myself out on the floor, tried to make myself comfortable on the hard boards.

I'd had a long day and I was tired. It wasn't all that difficult for me to sleep. But the thin strip of light gleaming from under their bedroom door disturbed me strangely. I knew I wouldn't go to sleep until it had gone out.

I didn't have to wait long. I heard the faint creak of bed springs, and a few seconds later a much heavier creaking as Freidman lifted his bulk on to the bed. Then abruptly, suddenly, the light snapped off.

I was almost asleep when it started.

I lay for a long while, wondering what it could be; a kinda low, continual whine.

I sat up, listened. There wasn't any doubt about it then. The noise was coming from their bedroom. I was fully awake now, listening intently.

I'd heard her speak only once, yet I knew instinctively it was her. She was murmuring a kinda low, whining murmur. I guessed they'd be talking about me and wondered what they'd be saying.

Stealthily, silently, I climbed to my feet, crept over to their door. I pressed my ear against the panels, listened intently.

I began to sweat.

I could hear much more distinctly now. She wasn't talking. She was moaning. Giving little moans, punctuated with sharp gasps of pain. And it wasn't what it could have been; a man and his wife roughing each other up a little. She was suffering, really suffering. The moans were breaking through her self-control as she steeled herself against pain.

I stood there in a cold sweat. It was Freidman who was with his wife. What could I do about it? He was a guy twice the size of me, and his wife hadn't yet started screaming for help.

38

I tiptoed back to my rolled-up jacket, carried it into a corner as far away from the bedroom door as I could get and settled down again.

But I couldn't sleep. The moans went on forever, and I just couldn't sleep while they continued.

CHAPTER FOUR

I drifted off to sleep without knowing it, woke with the sun streaming in my eyes and Freidman standing over me, jabbing his bare toe into my ribs.

I blinked, sat up, shook my head to clear it.

He was wearing loose-fitting, faded blue jeans, supported around his waist by a wide belt and nothing else.

"Quarter to five," he growled. "What's the matter with you? Want to sleep all day?"

I climbed to my feet slowly, and he went back into his bedroom, re-emerged a few moments later with his boots in his hand and his shirt over his arm. The dame followed him meekly, eyes downcast, a servility in her attitude that was almost slavish. She was wearing the same black dress, and in the light of day I could see more clearly how thin and faded it was. I could see even more. It clung to her youthful contours faithfully, outlining her youthful breasts and the curves of her flanks with a faithfulness that was strangely stirring, almost as though she wore nothing beneath that dress.

Freidman closed the bedroom door carefully, double-locked it like he'd got the crown jewels stowed away in there. He said nothing, just pointed. And obediently, bare-footed, she went through into the kitchen.

He looked at me with hard eyes, stroked the night stubble that turned his heavy features blue, and said in a harsh voice: "Water, boy. Water for washing."

I drew the water from the well, and the three of us washed outside in the open, sharing the same bowl, and same towel. When I thought Freidman wasn't watching, I studied the girl carefully, tried to read in her face an explanation of the moans I'd heard the night before. It was difficult, because not once would she look at me directly. There were still the heavy shadows under her eyes, and the same, kinda weary droop to her shoulders. But beyond that, she appeared no different.

And from the time we finished washing, I had little time to think about anything except work.

It was just five o'clock when the baker arrived. I've never handled so many loaves at one time in my life before, and it seemed I was ceaselessly carrying armfuls of bread into the kitchen while Freidman stood watching us with sly eyes, supervising every action.

Already the sun was up, and already the heat was beginning to make itself felt.

Our day started with cutting the loaves into slices. I wanted to help, but Freidman stopped me with a scowl. "She does the work in the kitchen," he growled. "Don't interfere."

There was nothing to do then for a time but stand and watch while she cut the slices, spread them with butter.

"Soup and coffee," said Freidman.

Obediently she went over to the stove, switched it on.

The milkman arrived. I went outside, handled the huge containers that had to be brought into the kitchen, emptied their contents into another container. It was twenty to six when the milkman left.

And the heat in the kitchen was beginning to increase now. The coffee and the soup were simmering, sending drifting vapour clouds up towards the ceiling. The sun was beating down on the iron roof, baking the air inside, turning it into an unbreakable inferno.

The dame was beginning to feel the heat. Her face was damp and shiny and the sweat patches under her arm-pits began to show.

Freidman jerked his head at me to follow, led the way out from the kitchen, went behind the counter and showed me the service hatch that opened on to the kitchen. Then he settled himself comfortably in a chair behind the counter and waited.

A little after six o'clock, they started arriving. Cab drivers, salesmen travelling across the States with their sample cases, travellers going places in a hurry and making an early stop on the road, and tired truckers who'd been driving all night.

41

And from the time it started, it was non-stop, tough going all the time.

Freidman sat behind the counter at the cash till, watching every move I made. I had to take the customers' orders, bellow them through the hatch, carry the order to the table as I received it from Freidman's wife and collect the cash. Freidman's sly eyes watched everything. He told me how much to collect, and I had I to take the dough straight back to him, collect the change, if any.

It was easy to see why this dump did such a brisk trade. It was thirty miles from anywhere, and on a hot, dry and thirsty road. Travellers got the feeling they'd met up with an oasis.

I kept hard at it, carrying plates of sandwiches, soup and coffee and soft drinks to the perspiring customers, returning the empty and dirty plates and thrusting them through the hatch.

How Freidman's wife managed to cope with it all was a mystery. There was coffee to be brewed, sandwiches to be cut, plates and cups to be washed, and it went on and on, a never-ending stream of orders.

It wasn't until just after two o'clock that we got a short respite.

There was a sprinkling of customers in the dining room. Freidman looked at me, said in a gritty voice: "I figure the water tank's empty. Better fill it up."

I went through into the kitchen, and the heat of it nearly knocked me back. I'd been sweating before; now the sweat began to run out of me.

The dame was standing over by the sink, her haunches pressed up against it as though to absorb its coolness, her head drooping on her chest like she was asleep while standing up.

When I opened the door, she started like a frightened horse, kinda flinched, stared at me with wide eyes full of apprehension.

That was the first time I'd seen her eyes. They were big and brown, soulful and full of apprehension. It was a relief to see fear dissolve from those eyes and relief take its place.

"The water tank," I said. "I've got to fill the water tank."

She nodded, switched her eyes away from mine quickly, moved to one side so I could get at the buckets underneath the sink. And the heat in there was appalling, oppressive, heavy and sticky. I didn't know how she managed to work hard in all that heat. When I bent to get the buckets, I was so close to her I could have touched her. Her black hair was damp like she'd dipped it in water, her forehead and cheeks glistened with perspiration and the sweat patches beneath her arms, extended and embraced her breasts. Her damp frock was sticking to her belly and her thighs like she'd cooled herself with water.

I straightened up with the buckets in my hands, pushed past her and tried to catch her eyes. Deliberately, she turned her head away from me. I carried on, walked out through the kitchen door, made for the stone well.

Out in the open, it was even worse. The sun beat down like a death ray, burning and torturous. In the few minutes it took me to draw water from the well, I was feeling giddy, had to sacrifice half a bucket of water to soak my head, freshen myself up.

When I got back to the kitchen, a new order had arrived, and she was working again, standing at the table, slicing bread for sandwiches with an experienced deftness. It was steaming hot in that kitchen, and working hard without a break the way she was, was worse than stone breaking in jail. As I passed behind her, I saw the sweat patches on her shoulders and back, could almost feel the perspiration trickling down her legs.

It needed ten buckets of water to fill that tank, and long before I was through, Freidman was yelling at me through the hatch to put a move on.

A little later on, Freidman's wife prepared sandwiches and coffee for us, and then towards the end of the afternoon, the traffic began to dwindle, die away to nothing.

It was dusk when Freidman switched on the "Closed" sign, indicating work was through for the day.

As far as the customers were concerned, that is!

I still had to sweep and scrub out the joint, draw more water from the well, while Freidman's wife cleaned up the kitchen, made everything bright and shiny the way he liked it.

Freidman and I had our evening meal together in the dining room. His wife passed it through the hatch to us, just like we were two more customers. There was nothing cooked, the same as the night before; ham, cheese and pickles. But I'd worked so hard, I was ravenously hungry, found it as satisfying a meal as I'd ever eaten.

That night, the routine was exactly the same as it had been the previous night. Freidman sat in a chair opposite me and read the newspaper, leaving me to shuffle my feet. When his wife had finished her work in the kitchen, she joined us and sat in silence for half-an-hour until Freidman climbed to his feet, looked at his watch and jerked his thumb towards the bedroom door.

Obediently, she climbed to her feet, followed him to the bedroom door, waited while he opened it up, and then slipped quickly inside. Freidman didn't even say good-night. He followed her inside, and I heard the bolts being shot.

I knew what was expected of me.

I rolled up my jacket, placed it as a pillow on the floor, turned off the lights, and stretched myself out in the darkness.

I was beginning to understand a great many things now. It was convenient for me to stop with Freidman and help him. But it was mighty convenient for Freidman too.

He hadn't done a stroke of work all day, except collect dough, which can be a pleasure. He'd just sat comfortably behind the counter while his wife slaved in the kitchen and I worked in the dining room.

Sure, it was a nice set-up for Freidman. But I wasn't gonna stand it for long. Only just so long as it suited me to stay.

I couldn't understand why Freidman's wife kept taking it. If she was his wife, that is. Because apart from her wedding ring and the fact they shared the same bedroom, there was nothing to suggest they were man and wife. She was half his age, and not much more than a slave. In the twenty-four hours I'd been there, I hadn't heard him talk to her once, except to issue an order. She hadn't talked at all, just meekly, obediently obeyed his instructions.

Yeah, it was a strange set-up. Made even stranger by the attitude of Freidman towards his wife, an attitude completely devoid of sympathy, affection or kindliness.

There was another strange thing, too, I'd noticed. The way he carried the key of their bedroom in his pocket, as though he had something locked away there that the world shouldn't see. And I'd noticed that during the day, not once had the dame gone to the bedroom. It was as though the kitchen was her province for the day, where she was compelled to remain, and the bedroom her prison for the night.

I turned uncomfortably on the hard, wooden boards, wished there was a groove into which I could fit my hip. I'd had a long and heavy day, and I'd have to be up early again in the morning. I closed my eyes, felt the lethargy of sleep begin to overtake me.

And then, very gently, very softly, it began; fainter than it had been the night before, but noticeable immediately because my nerve centres were reverberating, receptive, waiting for it. She was still whimpering when I fell asleep.

CHAPTER FIVE

Every day it was the same routine, up early in the morning, Freidman ushering his wife out of the bedroom and carefully locking it behind them, the three of us washing outside in the open air, and then the mad, blind rush to cope with the steady flow of customers while the hot sun beat down remorselessly and the dry earth shimmered in the heat.

And all the time, Freidman's attitude gave me a queer feeling in my belly. He never spoke except to issue orders, and his wife never said a word. But I sensed all the time that Freidman was watching me and his wife with a kinda cruel, detached, scientific interest. And the fourth day I was there, I saw something that explained a great deal.

It was towards the end of the day, when the stream of customers had dwindled to a solitary truck driver. I'd been drawing water from the well, and stumbled up the steps to the kitchen with a loaded bucket in each hand, feeling weak and light-headed from the heat of the sun.

Freidman was standing over his wife, staring down at her with hard, bitter eyes as she gathered up the pieces of a shattered cup. I could see apprehension in the slope of her shoulders and the way her head hung.

She got to her feet slowly, timidly, went over to the dustbin, dropped the pieces inside.

Freidman watched her wordlessly, and as though her eyes were compelled by his, she turned her head, stared back at him.

Still without speaking, he pointed to the floor beside him, a silent order that she unwillingly obeyed, coming back to him with reluctant footsteps; dull, hopeless despair reflected in her brown eyes.

What happened then explained that nightly whimpering. He reached out for her, his thick, strong fingers gathering up the loose folds of flesh at her side. Her head went back and her body went rigid. I watched with a kinda stupid surprise and horror inside me as Freidman's fingers pinched mercilessly.

The most amazing thing of all was the way she stood submissively while he did it, as though she'd learned there was no escape, only a meek acceptance of pain.

Her body arched in the rigidity of pain, her eyes rolled towards the ceiling, the skin of her jaw stretched tight and her mouth opened in a silent scream as her lips writhed.

Freidman's face was grim with the effort he was exerting, perspiration beading his forehead. I could see the knuckles of his fingers turning white with the pressure he exerted, and then slowly and mercilessly he twisted his hand.

That was when the whimpering began. It didn't seem to come from her mouth. It seemed to come out from deep down inside her, whistling out over her teeth, a kinda animal noise. There was cotton-wool in my belly, and my knees were rubbery, unable to take my weight. Her head was right back on her shoulders now, her mouth with its writhing lips wide open and her arched body as rigid as though it was made of steel. And the strange thing was, she still made no attempt to break away. It was even worse than hearing her whimper.

I sweated in the grip of conflicting emotions. Fear, horror, hatred, disgust and loathing. I wanted to do something to stop this horribleness, but didn't know what I could do. And while I stood there staring, open-mouthed, my limbs weak and boneless, Freidman's eyes found mine, grinned maliciously. He grated, "Don't waste time here, son. The customers are waiting. Get going."

His harsh voice broke the spell. I found the strength come back to my legs, found I was obeying him, only too anxious to get out and away from that kitchen. I closed the door behind me, and even out in the dining room, I could still hear a faint whimpering.

Two more customers entered at that moment, gave their orders. I went over to the hatch, opened it up and shouted through the orders. Maybe a coupla minutes later, Freidman came out from the kitchen, mopping his sweating forehead with a grimy handkerchief. His eyes deliberately searched for and found me.

47

I knew he was watching me, but I couldn't face him. I deliberately made myself preoccupied with work. But all the time, he was watching me, and at last I couldn't resist any longer. My eyes slowly climbed to his, stared at him unwillingly.

There was a kinda greedy, crazed, calculating expression in his eyes, as though he was gauging my reactions, laughing at me and at some malicious private joke of his own.

And as though the pattern of my life was being irresistibly fashioned in that cafe, something else happened that same night that erased from my mind any doubts I might have had about Freidman's cruelty.

I'd swept and scrubbed out the dining room and was sitting with Freidman, fidgeting, but not too obviously, surreptitiously watching his strong fingers as he leafed through the newspaper he was reading.

He said, abruptly: "Get me a glass of milk, will you?"

I was learning quickly. I said, "Yes, sir," promptly climbed to my feet, strode over to the kitchen door.

It was the first time I'd been through to the kitchen after the joint had closed for the evening. But I was in and out of there so many times during the day, it didn't occur to me to knock.

It musta been her frock she was washing, because she was bent over the kitchen sink completely naked. I heard the kitchen door swing shut behind me, heard the gasp of surprise rasp in her throat.

She spun around, eyes wide and terrified, pressing herself back against the sink. There was a hot, confused haze in my brain and, shocked by surprise, I stood there staring at her dumbly. And she stood there staring back, making no attempt to cover herself.

My eyes washed over her, absorbed every part of her with a kinda flushed innocence. And she still didn't move, stood there like she was paralysed.

I knew what I should do. I should turn on my heel quickly and return again after she'd had time to dress.

But that would necessitate giving Freidman an explanation, and the last thing I wanted was to tell Freidman I'd just seen his wife ... naked!

I had to try three times before I managed to get the words out. "He wants a glass of milk," I faltered. Then, with an effort, I tore my eyes away from her, walked over towards the larder.

It was as though averting my eyes released her. She lunged for a small hand-towel, kinda cowered behind it as she draped it to the best advantage. I didn't look at her again, but I could feel her eyes watching me all the time as I poured the milk, carried it across the kitchen and back to the dining room.

I almost sighed with relief when I saw Freidman hadn't moved from his chair. He took the glass from me without a word, not even looking up from his paper. And I was glad of that, because I wouldn't have liked him to see the expression in my eyes.

I went back to my chair, sat down and brooded sullenly.

Yet it was no business of mine. No-one would come between a man and his wife.

But I couldn't stop thinking about it, the way she'd been bent stooping over the sink, the way she'd turned to face me, and the way her white skin was blotched and marred by angry bruises and ugly red marks. I boiled inwardly as I thought about her. From immediately below her breasts, down to her hips, she wore a bodice of bruised, discoloured flesh that was a mute but graphic proof of how Freidman used his fingers.

I tried to catch her eyes when she came in to join us, but she kept her face averted. I noticed the care with which she settled herself in her chair, and knew now it was not from fatigue, but because of the pain of swollen and tender flesh, which nightly was bruised and punished by the monster who was her husband.

I looked at the dress, could see she had indeed washed it. Grease spots I had seen earlier had been cleaned away. The fact she could wear her dress so soon after washing it was just one more proof of how hot was that kitchen.

A little later, Freidman made the inevitable movements, yawned, glanced at his watch, climbed to his feet and motioned his wife towards the bedroom.

She stood at the door with her head hanging, hands at her sides, passively waiting for him to open up.

When the door had closed behind them, I rolled up my jacket, switched off the light, went outside on the sun porch, and stretched myself on the wooden boards.

I knew I'd be bitten by mosquitoes, that there was the risk a rattlesnake might find its way on to the veranda. But I couldn't continue listening to that whimpering sound night after night, especially now I knew how it was caused.

Somehow, I decided, I'd have to get away and get away quick. I didn't mind the work, although it was hard enough and unpaid.

But this other thing was driving me crazy.

I slumped with my head lolling forward, my shoulders hunched and my elbows resting on my knees. I felt sick, knew they were deliberately waiting, giving me time to recover.

The fat guy was standing in front of me. He rasped, "Lift your head up."

I made an effort, but my head was heavy like lead.

He put his fist beneath my chin, jabbed upwards so hard that my shoulders went back against the chair, my head snapping back, almost cracking my neck.

"You heard," he growled. "Hold your head up."

It was an effort, but I managed it.

His huge bulk was planted squarely in front of me, his rock-like fist threatening, a bitter loathing and hatred in his eyes. He gritted through his teeth like he was fighting hard to control his temper: "Your name is Farran, isn't it?"

"Yeah," I mumbled through lips that were split and puffed.

"And you killed Freidman for his dough, didn't you?" he rasped.

I didn't answer.

"You're a mad dog, a killer," he snarled. "You're not fit to live among decent men and women. Are you?"

I didn't answer.

His palm cracked across my cheek, rocking my head. I felt little pain; only numbness and the salty taste in my mouth. Blooded spittle trickled out from between my lips.

"That guy was good to you, wasn't he?" he growled. "Gave you a chance, gave you a job, took you into his own home and treated you like a son."

I didn't answer.

"And how do you repay him?" he rasped.

I still didn't answer.

"You killed him," he snarled. "Killed him like you'd kill a dog. Killed him so you could steal his dough."

My head was so heavy, beginning to fall forward again.

"And you stole his wife, too, didn't you, you swine? The guy opened his doors to you, and you killed him for his dough and his wife."

I was fighting hard, but my head was too heavy. It was falling lower and lower.

"You're a killer," he snarled. "A menace to society, a ruthless, merciless killer. You've got the savage instincts of a killer and the crazed mind of a killer. You killed Freidman, didn't you?"

I didn't answer, couldn't answer. My head was falling and I knew what was gonna happen, but could do nothing about it.

He straightened me with an uppercut that mashed my teeth together, pounded my shoulders against the back of the chair and sent me and the chair crashing backwards on the floor. Through a tunnel of blackness, I heard his voice repeating again and again:

"You stole his wife. You stole his dough. You killed him for his dough and his wife. You're a killer. A mad dog!"

CHAPTER SIX

I'd been there almost a week, working the same routine, working so hard I musta sweated away ten pounds.

And then, just after lunch when things were quiet, he broke the routine.

He looked at his watch, got up from his chair, fixed me with his mocking, black eyes. "You'll have to run the joint yourself for a while," he instructed. "I'm going into town. I'll be away three or four hours."

It was a blunt statement, and he didn't wait to see if I objected or not. It was an order he expected me to obey. He went to his bedroom door, dug down into his pocket for the keys. That was the first time I'd seen him enter the bedroom during the day.

A few more customers came in just then, and by the time I'd finished serving, he had come out from the bedroom and was carefully locking the door behind him.

He was wearing a faded jacket and carrying a small, battered attache case. He walked towards the door with slow, ponderous steps, stopped when he reached the door, looked over his shoulder and said, right out loud in front of the customers: "Watch the dough. I want every penny accounted for. And put up the 'Closed' sign if I'm not back in time. Get the place cleaned and swept."

I watched him surreptitiously from a window as he went around back of the house to the tumble-down shack where he garaged the car.

It was a Ford, maybe six years old, but it ran well enough. I watched him as he swung out on to the dusty highway and speeded off in the direction of Claremont.

More customers arrived then, and for the next hour I kept busy. Then, as often happened, business tailed off completely.

I sat in the dining room for maybe ten minutes without a soul in the place. Then I knew I couldn't fight against it any longer. I just had to talk to her.

I went through to the kitchen, and she was standing at the sink washing plates. As I stood in the open doorway staring at her, I could tell from the way she held her shoulders that she knew I was watching her.

It was hot in there.

Stifling hot!

The dining room had the windows open and was shaded by an almond tree. But the kitchen was an oven, pots boiling all the time, just one window and one door for ventilation, and a tin roof that musta been red hot beneath the bite of the sun.

I said, hoarsely: "It's killing in here."

I mightn't have spoken, for all the notice she took of me.

"Why don't you come out to the dining room for a breather?"

She still didn't answer.

I stood watching as she drew the washed plates from the sink, dried them on a tea-cloth. I could see the dark sweat patches on the back of her dress. It was clinging to her like she'd been swimming in it.

"He's gone," I said quietly.

"I know," she said, in her subdued voice, without looking up. "I saw him go."

"You scared of me, or something?" I demanded. "Why don't you look at me?"

She turned then; slowly, like it needed a tremendous will-power. Her brown eyes stared at me steadily, apprehensively. "Leave me alone," she said, in a low voice. "Why don't you leave me alone?"

It seemed like we were staring at each other for a hundred years. Inexplicably, my mouth was dry and I was sweating all over. She was young and I was young. We'd been living under the same roof together for almost a week and not so much as spoken a word to each other. All week I'd been tortured by the memory of her, the way I'd seen her that day, horrified eyes staring at me, forgetful of her nakedness. She'd been an irresistible appeal I couldn't put out of my mind.

53

I could tell from her eyes that she was remembering it too, remembering I'd seen her unclothed, looked at her in the way that only a man can look at a woman.

It burst out of me suddenly before I could stop it. "Why do you stay here?" I breathed. "Why do you let it continue?"

She said dully, numbly: "Why don't you leave me alone?"

"You don't have to take it," I blurted. I was suddenly reckless, determined she should understand what I was trying to tell her, not even caring in that moment if she repeated to Freidman what I said. "Why don't you clear out, run away from him. How long can you live this way, anyway? He'll kill you before long."

She said quickly, breathlessly, like just thinking about it was too risky: "Don't talk that way. Don't say those things."

"You're crazy to go on this way," I insisted. "It'll kill you. Morally and physically, it'll kill you. You just can't go on taking it."

I heard the doorbell clang as another customer entered. I went out quickly to get his order, yelled the order through the hatch and later served it. Then, when I'd collected the money and put it in the till, I went back to the kitchen again.

She was standing by the table now, half-sitting on it. It was the only way she could manage to rest a little. I could see through the thin dress how the heat and fatigue of the day caused her young breasts to droop and press damply against her bodice. She couldn't have been wearing anything beneath that dress. The way it clung to her, damp with perspiration, proved that.

She said tiredly, warningly: "Don't ever let him hear you talking this way."

"Why do you stay?" I persisted. "Has he got some hold over you, or something?"

"I've got no choice," she said, dully. She raised her arm to brush damp hair back off her glistening forehead, and I watched her skin flowing smoothly beneath the damp dress.

"Whatever happened, you couldn't be worse off than you are here," I insisted. "You're a slave here. Even guys in jail don't live this bad. You've got no liberty, you slave all day under impossible conditions, and at night ..." I broke off, flushed embarrassedly.

54

She knew what I meant. Without thinking, she gently rested her fingers upon her waist, as though trying to soothe pain. "It's no good," she said, in a dull voice. "There's nothing I can do."

I stared at her, willing her to understand. "There's plenty you can do. What's to stop you right now from going into your bedroom, packing your clothes and clearing out. It's as easy as that."

The doorbell jangled, and I slipped back into the dining room. It wasn't another customer. It was the last of the customers leaving.

I gathered up the dirty crockery, carried it over to the counter. I didn't go back into the kitchen right away. I deliberately waited, giving her a chance to think over the advice I'd given her.

After the hectic bustle of the day, the joint was quiet. No noise whatsoever came from the kitchen, just as though nobody was in there.

I waited ten minutes and then went over to the kitchen door, opened it wide. I stood on the threshold, holding the door open, letting the hot air waft out from the kitchen. I said: "This'll reduce you to a grease spot. There's no customers now. Step out here and grab yourself some air."

She was so subdued, so obedient to Freidman's every whim, I had the crazy idea that if she could break her routine, even in a small way like stepping out to the dining room to take a breather, it would break the control he exerted over her.

"Just for five minutes," I pleaded. "You've been here for twelve hours, working non-stop. Even guys in Sing-Sing are given the chance to breathe fresh air. Freidman isn't here to see you."

She kinda fought a battle inside herself, twined and untwined her fingers uncertainly, suddenly made a decision and came over towards the doorway, with slow, reluctant steps like she was taking a tremendous chance.

The fear of Freidman musta been embedded deep down inside her. She wouldn't come through into the dining room. She stood on the threshold, leaning against the door jamb, with one foot in the kitchen and one foot in the dining room.

She was panting a little, and her eyes kept flicking apprehensively towards the door.

And suddenly she looked so timid, so worn, so tired, and so pathetic, I forgot she was maybe three or four years older than me, felt protective and wanted to comfort her.

Her eyes rested on me, startled and wondering at her own daring. "It won't hurt if I stop here for five minutes, will it?" she asked, and her voice was pleading for reassurance.

"You could take a chair," I urged, "sit down comfortably and rest properly."

There was a hopeless expression in her eyes. "I couldn't do *that*," she whispered. "I'm not supposed to leave the kitchen, ever! If he found out, he'd be furious."

I stood in the doorway opposite her, the door jamb hard and sticky against my shoulders. "Have you thought over what I said?" I urged. "Are you going to leave here? Make a break for it?"

"I couldn't do it," she whispered, frightened. "I daren't."

"It's so easy," I urged. "You grab a suitcase, pack the few things you need, and scram. What little dough you need, you can take from the till. You'll be able to pick up another job easily, and you won't have to work a tenth as hard."

Her eyes flicked to the door, as though she was watching for Freidman, and then she looked down at the floor, shook her head slowly. "I couldn't do it," she whispered, "I couldn't do it!"

I looked down, noticed the way the damp dress clung to her parted thighs, the brownness of her bare legs and the sheen of sweat that made them glisten. Her bare feet gave her a healthy touch; she was like a young animal, healthy and vigorous.

Then suddenly I was remembering her the way I'd seen her that day, too startled to move, her naked body glistening with sweat as I stared at her with a kinda tormenting hunger unleashing itself inside me. I was glad she couldn't see my eyes, and I was startled by the increased pulsing of my heart, by the wild, crazy thoughts flooding into my mind.

"I can't leave," she said dully. "He's thought of everything."

"What's to stop you?" I demanded hotly. "Tell me just one thing that can stop you leaving?"

She said, dully, looking down at her feet: "A girl's gotta have clothes."

"Sure," I said. "Pack what you need and buy some more when you've earned some dough."

Her fingers plucked at the waist of her skirt. "This is the only dress I've got," she said, quietly.

I stared at her in amazement.

She lifted one bare foot, wriggled her toes. "I've no shoes," she added.

I gulped disbelievingly. "You mean that dress ... that's all you've got to wear? That's the only clothing you've got!"

"I couldn't get far with bare feet, one dress and no underclothes," she said bluntly.

I let breath whistle out slowly through my teeth.

She was a slave, a modern slave – without chains, it was true, but also without clothes. Lack of clothes shackled her to this snack bar as strongly as the most powerful chains.

A wave of pity swept over me. I saw the dark rims under her downcast eyes, the tired droop of her shoulders, the weariness and dejection expressed in every line of her body. I said, eagerly: "I'll help you. I'll get a job. I'll buy clothes, help you get away from here."

She shook her head, hopelessly. "It's no good. I can't get away. I shall never get away. It's the way he's made. He never lets anyone get the better of him. He'd find me somehow, pay detectives to search for me." She shuddered. "And when he found me, it'd be ten times worse."

"Are you married to him?"

She bit her lip, nodded without looking up at me.

"How could you marry a guy like that?" I protested. "He's old enough to be your father. A guy who treats you the way he does!"

"I guess he kinda bought me," she admitted, slowly. "It was when he owned another cafe fifty miles further south. I come from a large family, and we were poor, terribly poor. My father owns just a little ground, and it was a struggle to feed us all. Father used to sell eggs to Freidman, and I had to deliver them. That's how he got to know me."

"What d'ya mean?" I demanded. "What d'ya mean, he bought you?"

"He loaned land to my father," she said wearily. "Loaned father the money to buy more cattle, and took out debentures on the land. I was the price that had to be paid for his help."

That explanation made things much more understandable. "You didn't want to marry Freidman, then?"

"I had no choice," she said, dully. "So many mouths to feed at home, and things getting worse and worse every day."

"Did you know what Freidman was like before you married him?"

"I'd hardly ever spoken to him," she said, dully. "He was practically a stranger. We were married as soon as possible after he'd spoken to father, and immediately afterwards he bought this place, brought me over here."

She was quiet for a long while. Then she added: "I haven't seen my family since I was married, over a year ago."

Dejection and misery were apparent in every line of her body. Then, as I was watching her, a tear made a glistening trail down across her cheek.

I forgot where we were standing, forgot that a customer coming in the drive could see us through the window, forgot everything in the sudden wave of pity that swept over me. I put my arm consolingly around her, let her rest her head against my shoulder.

I could feel her shuddering as she tried to stop the sobs welling up from deep down inside her. Then, suddenly remembering where we were, she pushed away from me savagely and ran back into the kitchen.

I went after her, closing the kitchen door behind me, knowing the shop bell would ring if a customer came in. She was standing over by the sink with her back towards me, shoulders hunched and hands clenched tightly.

I walked over to her, spun her around, pulled her head down against my shoulder. She was somehow like a little dog that had been stoned, starved, beaten and chased. She was hungry for a little affection. She melted against me gratefully, and maybe for the first in many weeks or months, she let the sobs well out of her, let all the misery and the hopelessness and the depression bubble out in long, racking sobs that caused her shoulders to shake, her knees to tremble.

It was maybe five minutes before she got most of it out of her system, and all the time I was holding her tightly, comforting her. She was pathetically grateful for affection, nestled against me like her body was one great longing for human companionship. And as her sobs eased and she moved her face against my chest to dry her cheeks on my shirt, I felt the hotness of her skin through her damp dress, once again remembered abruptly the way I'd seen her that day, standing at the sink and staring at me with wide, frightened eyes, too startled to lift her hands to conceal her nakedness.

I could feel the hotness of her fingers through my shirt as she clutched my shoulders, and ideas I couldn't suppress were flooding into my mind with grim persistence. Without meaning it, I moved, and she was there, moving with me. My hands were around her waist, and the softness of her skin through the thin, damp dress was frightening and exciting.

I was holding her that way for maybe five minutes before we both realised at the same time that I was doing more than comfort her.

She wrenched away from me savagely, almost frantically, got around the other side of the table, stared across it at me with wild eyes that were also strangely puzzled.

I growled thickly, "What's the matter? You're not frightened of me are you?" and was surprised to find I was breathless.

She didn't say anything, just stared at me. The strong curves of her rounded breasts pressed through the damp dress, showing she was breathing rapidly.

"It's okay," I soothed hoarsely. "You don't have to be scared." I took three paces around the table, and she moved quickly, put the table between us again.

I'd only been in that kitchen a short time, but I was already feeling the heat of it. The sweat was streaming down my forehead, and my shirt was wet. "You don't have to be scared," I panted. "You don't have to be scared of me." My hands were tingling, still sensing the perspiration of her body through that damp dress.

She said in a hushed, frightened voice: "You mustn't do that. You mustn't ever do it again. If he found out, he'd kill us. He'd kill both of us. You mustn't come near me again ... ever!"

Seeing her like that, just across the table from me, so near and yet so far and telling me to keep away from her, inflamed the hot desire inside me.

I wanted her close against me, like she'd been a few moments earlier. I wanted to feel the softness of her body beneath her dress, feel the heat of her thighs beating against mine, feel her fingers digging hard into my shoulders.

"Come here just a minute," I pleaded. "Let me hold you again for just a minute!"

Her eyes were wild, and I could see desire fighting her fear. She said, in a whisper: "No!"

I moved again, slowly this time, circling the table in a way that wouldn't startle her. This time, she waited, watched me with wild, dark and frightened eyes.

I didn't quite reach her. The clanging of the shop bell seemed twenty times louder than normal, shattering the tenseness of the moment with an abruptness that was startling and sending her cowering away from me with wild fear flooding her eyes.

I took three swift strides across the room, pushed out through the kitchen door and almost died with relief when I saw it wasn't Freidman. Two truck drivers were settling down at a table.

But the shock of their arrival changed everything like a pail of cold water had been thrown over me. Almost as though I had absorbed some of her terror of Freidman.

I called their order through the hatch, waited there while it was prepared.

I would have to close the dining room pretty soon, and knew in advance I was gonna clean up the joint thoroughly, make it spick and span and keep well way from that kitchen.

Because Freidman was liable to come back any time now, and I had the sure conviction he'd do what she said he'd do.

Maybe even kill us if he caught us when we'd lost our heads.

My mind was muddy, my thoughts sluggish and the pain a white mist.

From a long way away, I heard a voice saying: "Better clean him up a bit."

There was peace then for a time, blessed peace while they allowed me to lie there with my mind groping through the pain towards consciousness.

Then they were there again, the clank of an iron bucket on the stone floor, my shoulders stabbing as they twisted me on to my back, a sponge heavy with water, sloshing into my face, washing away the blood and the vomit, bringing me nearer to consciousness and awareness of pain.

"Leave me alone," I pleaded tearfully. "Don't do it any more."

They grasped my arm, dragged me to my feet. My nerves were twisting and jumping, my body twitching with pain.

The fat dick said, viciously: "I'll be seeing you again soon, when you're in better shape."

I peered at him through that white mist, saw his cruel eyes and his flabby cheeks, and my mind tried to arch away from him.

A harsh voice grunted in my ear, "Cut that out," and excruciating agony jagged from my arm to my shoulder.

Everything was indistinct as they guided me through the door and back along the corridor to the familiar, stone cell. My lips tingled with numbness, and I knew they must be immensely swollen. One of my eyes was half-closed, too, kept watering. But they'd have an answer to all this, explain that I'd tried to escape and had to be forcibly detained.

They opened the door to my cell, hurled me inside so that I splayed forward, sprawling half across my bunk, outflung hands blindly groping to protect my tortured body from the hard callousness of the stone floor.

Then, as the slamming of the iron door clanged deafeningly in that small cell, I crawled on to my bunk, lay huddled there, my mind a tortured torment and my body one enormous and aching bruise.

I knew there was no way I could escape this torment. They neither needed nor wanted information. They wanted only that I should suffer and go on suffering.

61

And my tortured, pain-racked mind groped for understanding, found an answer that was not an answer. Freidman!

CHAPTER SEVEN

Freidman returned maybe an hour after I'd put up the "Closed" sign. I was still scrubbing the floor when his worn Ford crawled in around back of the shack, slashing the house with his headlights and giving warning of his return.

I knew she must have seen his headlights through the kitchen window, and I continued scrubbing the floor, my ears cocked, listening to the sound of his car being backed into the garage.

I'd locked the front door. There was only one way for him to come in – through the kitchen. And I was scared now, scared that maybe I'd gone too far and had talked too much, was scared the dame was so frightened of Freidman she might even tell him what had happened.

Apprehensively, I listened to his footsteps around back of the shack, the sound of his heavy boots grinding on the sill of the kitchen back door and the creak of boards beneath his weight. I didn't hear him speak, but he was in the kitchen maybe a minute.

Then the kitchen door opened and he stood framed there in the doorway, glaring down at me.

I looked at him, grinned weakly. My heart was thumping twice as fast as normal, and I was scared right down to my toes. I was telling myself I had to behave naturally, not allow him to think for one minute that anything had changed.

It was a strain. Because he stood squarely in the doorway, looking down at me with penetrating eyes that grinned malignantly, eyes that were slyly knowledgeable, almost suggesting he had seen and heard everything that had passed between me and his wife.

Then he said, quietly enough: "That's the idea, kid. Get the place cleaned up."

I bowed my head, put my shoulder behind the scrub-brush and worked hard to erase a tar stain that had been brought in by a truck driver's heavy boots. From the corner of my eye, I watched Freidman stride across to his bedroom door, change his faded, worn attache case from one hand to the other while he fumbled for the key.

He was in there only a moment, only long enough to deposit the attache case and strip off his coat. Then he emerged again, carefully locking the door behind him before striding heavily across to the kitchen hatch.

He opened it up, snarled through it harshly: "I want some food." Then he turned around, rested his elbows on the counter, and stared at me stonily.

That night passed the same as all other nights, except in one respect. I'd spoken to her, had made mental and physical contact with her. We shared a secret, a tiny fragment of her private life that she was able to retain to herself and prevent Freidman from taking. This secret was ours, something we shared, and that formed an intangible bond between us, that existed even although she never looked or talked to me, despite her mind and body being dominated by Freidman.

During the days that followed, I could feel the bond growing stronger, sense her when she was standing near me, and knew she could sense me in the same way. It was like we were both equipped with radar, able to detect and feel and converse silently with each other, although we were always yards apart.

Daily the bond became stronger, and when at night time I moved out on to the veranda, I could feel the seeds of angry, bitter resentment for Freidman growing inside me. Dimly, I realised the mounting anticipation inside me was the waiting for the day when Freidman would again take his shabby attache case and drive off, leaving us alone.

It was exactly a week later when Freidman announced he was going out. My heart was pumping madly as, between gathering up dirty crockery, I watched his grey Ford ease out from the garage, glide forward on to the main drag.

There were more customers than usual for that time of the day, and it was almost an hour and a half before I got my first opportunity to pass through into the kitchen.

She was standing over the hot sink, in the same, familiar and weary attitude. But there was a subtle difference now, a kinda stirring inside her when she heard me enter. She didn't turn around, although she knew I was there looking at her.

I went up behind her, rested my hands on her shoulders. She flinched, froze with a plate in her hands.

"We've got to talk," I said across her shoulder.

"You're crazy," she said fiercely. "This has got to stop. He'll kill us."

I gripped her shoulders more tightly, could feel her shrinking and shuddering. Quite suddenly, she let the plate slip back into the water.

"I've got it all figured," I said quickly. "I'm going to leave tomorrow. I'll get a job. I'll earn money. I'll earn the money to buy you clothes, get you out of here."

She shook her head slowly. "It's no good," she said, dully. "It's no good."

I placed my fingers on the nape of her neck. Her skin was wet and slippery with perspiration, her hair thick and damp. A quiver ran through her from head to toe.

"It's inevitable," I said urgently. "You've got to leave. It'll kill you if you carry on this way."

"You don't understand," she said weakly. "You just don't understand!"

I shifted my hands from her shoulders to her waist, crooked my fingers around her hip bones. She stood quite still, like she was fighting to control herself. I could almost see her skin through her damp dress, soft and milky.

"You don't have to do anything," I urged. "You don't need to run any risks. You just wait until I arrive one day when he's not around. I'll arrive with everything you need."

She lifted her hands out from the sink, brought them down over mine, held my fingers tightly like she was gonna pry them away from her, but pressing them hard against her instead.

She breathed a deep sigh, a sigh that expressed all the hopelessness inside her.

"It's no good," she said wearily. "He'll always find me. But it's more than that. It's what he'd do to my family. He owns the debentures on the land and can press for repayment any time he wants. He'd ruin my father, strip the family of everything, drive them into the gutter." She sighed. "I couldn't let that happen. I've just got to go on taking it."

I had to leave her then to deal with customers. I was busy for another half-an-hour, until business dwindled to nothing. Then once again I went back to the kitchen.

This time she turned around from the sink and faced me.

I went over to her. "We'll find a way," I said reassuringly. "You can't continue this way. It'll kill you."

"I guess you're a real nice guy," she smiled wryly, and brushed back a hank of damp hair that had fallen over her forehead. The movement strained taut the bodice of her dress, outlined the damp roll of her breasts and revealed a split in her underarm seam.

I stared at her, licked my lips.

She stared back.

I couldn't take my eyes off her.

She said, sharply: "Don't look at me like that."

I moved in on her, rested my hands on her hips, pulled hard so she was pressed up against me.

She said, in a pleading whisper: "Don't. We mustn't; it's crazy. He'll kill us." The palms of her hands were pressing against my chest. She coulda shoved me away if she wanted, but her arms lacked either the strength or the desire.

What she said was true. This was crazy. If Freidman knew, he would probably kill us. And we weren't even being smart. The door to the kitchen was wide open, and anyone could walk in on us from the dining room.

It was partly the danger that excited me. But most of it was the hot dampness of her pressing hard against me, the yearning for affection glowing in brown eyes that had reflected so much misery.

"This really means something. You and I," I breathed. "We've hardly spoken, but you and I both know it means something."

"You mustn't talk this way," she said faintly.

All the time, she was pressing hard against me so I could feel the hot blood pulsing through her, the urgent desire inside her, the weakness of hands that should have pushed me away. Her ripe lips were moist, half-parted.

I was enveloped in a hot haze, the sudden urgency of her making me tingle all over. Almost without knowing I was doing it, I ran my fingers along her spine, felt her quiver deliciously. When my fingers reached the nape of her neck, I grasped her damp hair, twisted her hair around my hand, pulled on it almost brutally, levering her lips forward to meet mine.

She could have stopped me any time. She knew it was crazy, and I knew it. I needed just one warning to make me draw back and hover on the brink instead of launching myself down into the yawning chasm.

She could have pushed me away with her hands.

She could have kicked.

She could have screamed.

But she didn't!

And from the moment her lips met mine, we were both falling; falling together, plunging downwards in an embrace that was almost savage. Her teeth were biting into my lip so deep that I felt a spasm of delicious pain, and I was hurting her too, hurting her in a way Freidman never hurt her. And the writhing of her body against mine was kindling the flame inside me to white-hot intensity.

Just a simple embrace and a simple kiss. But it had all the intensity and urgency of a high climax. And it was timeless, going on forever.

When the door from the dining room swung open and a harsh voice bellowed, "Hey!" it took seconds to float back to earth.

I backed away from her, sweating, red-faced and panting, still kept one arm around her as I faced the doorway.

He was a trucker, a big guy with an unshaven chin and wearing a black leather flying jacket. I saw his sharp eyes taking in everything, and the coarse, sly grin crossing his lips and curling them cynically. He was a regular customer and knew Freidman. He didn't have to draw me a picture so I should know what he was thinking.

He said, wickedly: "How about a little service, bud? Or do I have to wait until the big fella gets back?"

She was trembling as she pushed herself away from me, went back quickly to the sink.

67

"Just coming," I said, hoarsely, and crowded him out of the room, guided him over to a table.

He was the only customer, and he must have come unheard because the door hadn't been closed properly.

He gave me his order and I went over to the hatch, shouted it through to her. He had his eyes on me all the time. I was shaky and trembly. I stood behind the counter, trying to make up my mind what I should do. Finally, I took a deep breath, went over to him, looked at him levelly. "You're a regular, aren't you?" I said, and my heart was pounding painfully.

He was a big guy. He lounged back lazily in his chair, hooked his thumbs in his belt and grinned at me knowingly. "Sure thing," he agreed. "But you're kinda new around here."

I flushed uncomfortably. "Customers don't usually come pushing into the kitchen," I said.

He looked me up and down slowly with eyes that were just the tiniest bit annoyed. "You wouldn't be criticising, son, would you?"

It came out with a rush. I said, "You're the kinda guy who knows what time it is. Maybe you saw something. Maybe you only thought you saw something. But a guy who talks can cause an awful lot of harm. There's nothing can stop a guy talking if he wants to. But unless somebody's twisting his arm, there's nothing to make him talk."

He looked at me shrewdly. "Worried, huh?"

"That's it. I'm worried."

He straightened out, rested his elbows on the table, stared up at me and closed one eye knowingly. "It's this way, son," he said. "I've often wondered who worked there in the kitchen. She looks like a nice dish. You ain't got a thing to worry about. I'd do the same. When the boss was away, I'd try to make her as well. You don't have to worry. I ain't talking."

"It isn't that way at all," I said hurriedly. "It was just that she didn't feel well, and I was ...."

He winked again, a man to man wink. "Sure," he drawled. "I know. You were comforting her. But if the boss thinks there's anything going on, you both get the sack. I know. You don't have to worry, kid. I've sense enough to keep my mouth shut."

68

There were two knocks on the service hatch. I said, hurriedly: "That's your order now," and hurried to get it.

I loitered around back of the counter while he ate, and it seemed he would never finish. He was the only customer in the dining room, and I wanted to get him out of the way before more arrived. He seemed to take hours eating a sandwich, and it seemed he'd never finish drinking his coffee. When he lit up a cigarette and reached for a newspaper, I was trembling, unable to stand still, my nerves ragged.

I was so agitated that I forgot to charge him. He had to call me over, ask what he owed.

There was a twinkle in his eyes. He said, "Don't let her get you down, son. The job's the most important. Lose your job and you'll lose the dame."

I followed him out on to the veranda, watched him clump down the steps, cross over to his lorry and climb up into the driving seat. There was maybe an hour to go before closing time. But I turned back into the dining room, closed the door, locked it and switched on the "Closed" sign.

She was waiting for me, her eyes anxious and apprehensive, as I closed the door behind me. It was as though she didn't know whether to run to me or away from me.

I knew we were crazy. But I also knew nothing was gonna stop it happening. It was inevitable, something that had to happen, like a car going down hill with no brakes and no means of stopping until it hit bottom.

I walked over to the kitchen door, closed it deliberately, bolted it firmly. There were shabby, sun-dried and sun-bleached curtains that I drew, covering the glass portion of the door.

When I turned around, she was staring at me with a kinda wild, desperate look in her eyes. "You can't," she panted. "You mustn't. There's folk coming in all the time."

I crossed to the only window the kitchen possessed, jerked the curtains across, leaving us in a kinda half-light.

She shrank away from me, pushed herself back against the table.

I went over to her, stood squarely in front of her. "We can't stop this thing," I said hoarsely. "It's no good trying to fight against it."

"No," she panted. "You mustn't." There was a thoroughly scared note in her voice.

It was like it was before, the palms of her hands against my chest but without the strength to push me away. And with the door closed and the sun beating down on the iron roof, that kitchen was boiling us in our own perspiration, every tiny movement causing sweat to run from every pore.

"You mustn't," she whispered. "It's crazy. Anybody can come in."

My shirt was wet, sticking to me like I'd been rain drenched. I could feel beads of sweat forming, trickling down between my shoulder blades, running down my chest. I could feel her skin through the dress, hot and slippery, soft and desirable, the quickening of her breathing increasing the fierce urgency inside me. I did what I'd done before, ran my fingers along her spine, grasped her hair, pulled her lips to mine.

This time, she resisted, not too strongly, but enough. "Don't be crazy," she breathed. "Anyone can come in."

"I've locked the dining room," I whispered. "Closed down for the night."

I felt the tenseness inside her, the rigidity of shock and fear. "You can't," she whispered. "You can't do that and ..."

I forced her head towards mine, cut off her words with my mouth. Her rigidity lasted for maybe a coupla seconds, and then she was responding with a savage urgency that was almost frightening, grasping me fiercely, greedily. Her hands were as slippery as mine, and the very fury of her passion was frightening in its intensity, sweeping me along with it.

I was like we were fighting each other. She writhing and biting, me clutching her tightly, our hands seeking and finding each other almost brutally.

She panted, frantically: "No, you mustn't." But she wouldn't let me go, and the rim of the table was at the back of her thighs, bracing her, giving her resistance.

There'd never been anything like it for me before. I knew that there was no stopping now, that this just had to be.

She panted again: "No, you mustn't." Yet her fingers were in my hair, pulling me towards her, her hands caressing my sweat-soaked shoulders and her lips searching greedily

70

for mine.

Her dress tore. She grunted, panted: "No!" Then a few seconds later: "No! It's crazy."

I didn't say anything. I wasn't even thinking. Everything was a hot whirl of emotion, a perspiring whirlpool that grasped me in a delirious embrace, sucking me ever and ever down and down, my senses swimming with ecstasy as I plunged even more deeply towards the tranquility and peace I would find when the urgent, heady whirling ceased.

* * *

Maybe it was the heat in the kitchen, but all the strength was sucked out of me. I felt weak and dazed as I walked unsteadily to the kitchen door, unlocked it, swung it open. The hot air outside seemed almost fresh as I stumbled across to the well, lowered the bucket.

I was so weak, I was afraid I would never get the bucket to the top. And when I did, it seemed I would never get the bucket free from the hook and find the strength to swing it clear of the stone parapet.

The water was ice-cold. Plunging my head into it was like taking a header into an Alaskan lake. It was a physical shock that made me gasp, made me feel even weaker, so that I had to take a grip on myself to fight off an advancing grey mist. Then, as the shock of the cold retreated, my senses became clearer, my hearing more acute, the objects around me sharper and more clearly defined, my mind crystal clear and as sharp as a razor.

Slowly and thoughtfully, I sluiced myself down, washed away the sweat clogging the pores of my skin. Then I up-ended the bucket over my head, went back to the kitchen dripping wet, my hair a tangled mass hanging down over my forehead.

She was standing inside the kitchen, waiting for me, anxious and apprehensive.

And everything was different now!

I let my eyes wash over her, saw her differently, noticed she was maybe a little over-plump, that she had just the slightest suggestion of a double chin.

71

She whispered breathlessly: "It was crazy. We shouldn't have done it. Supposing he had come back."

I didn't say anything. I walked over to the window, jerked back the curtains and let the sun stream in.

She said: "He'd kill me if he found out. Whatever happens, you've got to stand by me. You understand that. You've got to stand by me." Her voice was shrill, almost fierce.

"Okay," I growled. "I'm here, aren't I? I offered to help you get away, didn't I?"

She lifted up her arm, revealing the underarm split now extending nearly to the waist. "Supposing he gets suspicious of this," she demanded, with a trace of hysteria in her voice. "Supposing he asks questions. What I am going to tell him?"

Every minute, I was realising more how crazy I'd been. I could see things differently now. It was almost as though sluicing myself in cold water had washed away all my hot, emotional and crazy ideas. I was wishing I'd stayed out front all the time, never entered the kitchen, never spoken to her.

"You've got to stand by me," she said petulantly. "You know what I mean. Anything might happen. And if he suspects you've ... he'll kill us."

I was crazy to have worked for Freidman, and I should never have let an affair go this far. The smart thing was clear out now, slip out quietly one night while Freidman and she were asleep.

And as though she could read my mind, she said abruptly: "You mustn't leave me. Not now. Understand? And if you go, you'll be sorry for it. I'll tell him something! Anything! I'll make him furious. I'll tell him you did it when I didn't want. Tell him you forced me."

A reaction had set in with her, a reaction of fear and hysteria. She wasn't herself, maybe had been walking on the knife-edge of hysteria for so long that her nerves were easily unbalanced.

"Don't be so crazy," I growled. "Of course I'm going to stay. What gives you the idea I'm gonna quit?"

"The way you're looking at me," she accused. "It's as though you hated me."

"Don't be crazy," I said again. "You're so scared of Freidman that you're getting silly ideas." Yet at the same time, I couldn't meet her eyes, and she knew it.

She said, in a tearful voice: "Supposing he finds out?"

"He won't find out," I said confidently. I squared my shoulders. "The only thing that'll give him ideas is if you continue acting this way." I jerked my head towards the kitchen sink. "Get cleaned up, will you? We've got to make up for lost time. Get the place cleaned up the way he wants. When he comes back, act normally, just the way you always act."

I drew another bucket of water, went through to the dining room, began to clean it out.

I was still cleaning when Freidman returned. This time, he stood in the doorway looking at me for a long while before I remembered to act normally, raise my eyes to his and give him a sickly grin.

CHAPTER EIGHT

Freidman suspected. I was certain of it.

I could sense it in his manner, in the way he looked at me and the way he looked at her.

But I also knew better. Freidman didn't know, couldn't know, and didn't suspect. It was my own guilt working inside me that made me imagine he was different. There had always been a strangeness about him, his all-knowing, malicious grin that was a promise of retribution.

I convinced myself that my guilty conscience was playing upon my imagination.

As he had done before, Freidman disappeared into the bedroom, came out again without the battered attache case. Then he went behind the counter, called for food through the service hatch, then started checking the day's takings in the till.

All the time he was counting, I could sense his eyes watching me, sly, calculating and malicious. When he was through checking the dough, he sat behind the counter eating steadily, his eyes boring into me, watching every movement I made, like he was a time, motion and fatigue inspector in a factory.

I was about through cleaning the floor when he called abruptly. "Hey, son!"

I looked up quickly, startled, eyes hunted, a hot flush making my face burn. His eyes were grinning at me, probing, penetrating deep into my soul, and his thin lips had an ugly twist.

"Another glass of milk," he instructed.

I couldn't look at him directly. I climbed to my feet, wiped my hands on my pants, collected his empty glass and passed through into the kitchen.

She scared me, because she was so guilt conscious. She looked at me fearfully, her face revealing the hidden terror inside her.

I narrowed my eyes at her warningly, crossed the kitchen, poured a fresh glass of milk. She turned back to the sink, kinda hunched her shoulders so her damp hair hung, half-concealing her flushed cheeks.

Then I saw it. It stood out a mile. It was so obvious that for a moment my heart stopped beating. The upper part of the kitchen door, which was of glass, still had the curtain drawn.

Normally it was never drawn.

I didn't stop to think. I was there in three quick strides, jerking the curtain back into its usual position, feeling my heart start beating again.

Then I knew I was crazy, that I shouldn't have touched the curtain. Because I could feel his eyes boring into the back of my neck, knew he was reading my brain, picking over it like a dame sorting clothes in a bargain basement, reading my innermost thoughts and gloating over them.

I spun around and he was there, framed in the doorway between the kitchen and the dining room, his eyes glinting with sardonic amusement and a malicious twist to his lips that sent cold shivers running down my spine.

He said, in a voice so soft it was more frightening than a harsh bellow: "That my milk you've got there, son?"

"Yeah," I said faintly. "This is it."

"Let's have it!"

I forced myself to walk over to him, try to act normally. There was a great fear leaping inside me, because I was now sure that he knew, that he'd seen me rip back the curtain and understood exactly why I had drawn it.

My heart was pounding painfully, every nerve and muscle inside me tensed, so that when he reached out, I flinched.

But it was the milk he wanted. Instead of the punishing, battering-ram impact of his fist, he took the glass from me and drank from it steadily, his eyes boring into me the whole time.

I wanted to flash her a quick glance to warn her she must keep herself under control, not to do anything out of the ordinary. But his eyes locked with mine, held tightly, probing, penetrating and frightening. Then, when he'd drained the glass, he handed it back to me, twisting his thin lips as he ordered: "Another glass, son."

He turned back into the dining room, deliberately left both of us alone while I drew the milk.

I didn't look at her. It was too dangerous. And I was so nervous that I spilt some of the milk on the floor.

Yet it was my own feeling of guilt that made me jumpy. Because when I got back to the dining room, he was seated comfortably at the table, reading a newspaper. He didn't even look up when I gave him the glass of milk, just nodded to show he knew it was on the table at his elbow.

After that, it was like every other evening. When she was through working in the kitchen, she came into the dining room, sat down at a discreet distance from Freidman with her hands in her lap and her eyes downcast.

Yet tonight there was a difference in the atmosphere. I wasn't looking at her and she didn't look at me. But it was like my nerve-ends were reaching out and touching her, sensing her, feeling the frightened vibrations inside her, knowing she was as acutely conscious of me as I was of her.

It was painful, sitting there that way. I wanted to be alone, have a chance to reason with myself, think things out slowly.

Maybe it was my imagination, but Freidman seemed to be reading that paper longer than usual. I breathed a sigh of relief when at last he dug down in his pocket, consulted his watch, stretched himself and climbed to his feet.

She got up, meekly and obediently, eyes downcast and hands at her sides.

He said, in a sharp voice: "Just a minute. Raise your left arm."

Her eyes climbed slowly to his, and there was a kinda numbed terror in them.

"Raise your arm when I tell you," he snarled, suddenly vicious.

She moved her arm like it was stuck to her side with invisible glue that wasn't quite set.

The underarm split in the seam of her dress extended almost to the waist. She'd found a pin, used it to the best advantage. But the seam gaped, revealing white skin, underarm hair and the bruised, discoloured flesh above the hip.

He demanded, brusquely: "How did you do that?"

"Please," she said, tearfully, her voice almost a sob. "It isn't a tear. It's just the seam."

"What do you want I should do?" he growled, harshly. "Buy you a new dress?"

Her eyes dropped, and as she stared down at her bare feet, it looked like she was trying to swallow a sob.

"You've got to make clothes last. Understand?" he demanded.

She nodded numbly, bitterly. I almost expected to see a tear glistening on her eyelashes.

"That's all," he grunted. "Bed."

There was a bitter ache inside me as I saw her pad over to the bedroom door with eyes downcast, head hanging, every line of her body expressing dejection.

Then I sensed his eyes boring into me, malicious and penetrating. "You ain't getting any ideas about leaving here just yet awhile, are you, son?"

I looked at him quickly, saw the knowledge in his eyes, licked my lips nervously. "No," I said, faintly.

"No what?"

"No, Sir," I said, promptly.

"That's fine," he sneered, with malicious satisfaction. "Because I've been hearing things, and I'm not the kinda guy who likes talking to cops and having them tramping all over the place asking questions."

After he'd closed the bedroom door behind him, I stood staring at it with grim terror numbing my heart. I'd maybe have gone on standing there for hours if the whimpering hadn't started.

That kinda broke the tension. I switched off the lights, went out on to the veranda, settled myself on the hard wooden boards and buried my head in my arms.

That was the first time I'd cried in many years.

* * *

77

I should have been smart, taken a risk and cleared out that same night. There was nothing to stop me except Freidman's veiled threats.

The next day, it was worse. Because not only did I have the guilty feeling that Freidman was watching me surreptitiously, but the dame herself wasn't being very clever.

She'd changed in some subtle way. She still looked tired and exhausted. But she had a kinda new vitality, like she could now see some distant horizon and a ray of hope. It wasn't anything you'd notice easily. You felt it rather than noticed it. But it was there all the time. And she did crazy things, too, deliberately letting her arm brush against me when I passed, catching my eye when Freidman wasn't looking, watching me, kinda stroking me with her eyes across the room.

The following day was hell for me. Guilt was strong inside me and intensified the feeling that Freidman's penetrating eyes were watching every move I made. I was convinced he couldn't fail to notice her subtlely changed manner, and expected every minute that Freidman would show his hand, demand a showdown.

That's what a guilty conscience does for you.

The second day wasn't so bad.

The third day, I knew everything was my imagination. Freidman didn't suspect a thing.

Then, with my fears at rest, my dormant desires began to strengthen.

She was there all the time, day and night, never more than a few yards from me, and I could sense her all the time, knew what she was thinking, knew she wanted me as I needed her. I was remembering the feel of her hot, damp skin, the urgency of her strong, young body thrusting against me, the salty taste of her lips and even the sour scent of her perspiration.

I found I was watching her when Freidman wasn't looking at me, observing the soft, liquid flow of her body beneath the dress, while desire was spreading and growing bigger and bigger inside me until it was torment.

It got so I couldn't stop thinking about her, remembering the creamy whiteness of her breasts, the tips of her fingers gouging into my back, the wide belt of discoloured, bruised flesh that made her quiver with delicious pain at the slightest touch, and the strength of her parted thighs.

It got so I couldn't sleep at nights. I was tormented by mental images of her, by overwhelming desire and the knowledge that all the time she was never more than a few yards away from me. Time couldn't pass quickly enough.

It seemed the day would never come, and when it did, the morning lasted an eternity. It needed a conscious mental effort to concentrate on my work, avoid mistakes that would focus Freidman's attention upon me.

And when finally Freidman went to his bedroom, unlocked it, and emerged with the familiar brown attache case, I was so nervous that my hands were trembly.

From the window, I watched him go around back to the wooden shack that was the garage, watched him edge his car out on to the road and drive off in the direction of Claremont.

And then the waiting was over!

I didn't go immediately to the kitchen. I kept on working, forced myself to go on working, wouldn't let my mind dwell on her, suppressed that hot, emotional desire inside me.

The next coupla hours seemed to last an eternity.

Then I got my opportunity. There were only three customers in the dining room, and they all left at the same time.

It was early, far too early. But I didn't hesitate. I locked the door after them, switched on the "Closed" sign and then walked slowly towards the kitchen door. My heart was pumping madly and my palms were sweating. But there was a calmness inside me now as well; the calmness of confidence and assurance.

She was waiting for me, expecting me. As I came through the kitchen door, she backed up slowly again the kitchen sink, stood with her haunches rammed hard against it as though she needed support.

I said: "I've closed the shop!"

She didn't say anything, just watched me with hot eyes that were scared and hungry at the same time.

79

I moved over towards her slowly, stood in front of her. Even before I touched her, her breathing quickened, something happened to her eyes so they seemed loose, liable to roll freely in their sockets.

I said, hoarsely: "I've been thinking about you all the time, and the way it was. I keep thinking about you, and it's driving me mad."

She closed her eyes, clenched her hands tightly, like she was exerting all her will-power. She whispered: "The curtains. Quick. The curtains."

I closed the back door of the kitchen, locked it, pulled the curtain. Then I pulled the curtains over the window. Already the heat in that kitchen was beginning to get me, the sweat seeping out of me, making me feel faint.

I went back to her. She was standing the way she'd been standing when I left her. I reached out, gently removed the pin that inadequately fastened the split in her dress. As my fingers brushed her side, she flinched, caught her breath. It coulda been a gasp of pain or ecstasy.

"I couldn't wait for today," I panted.

She launched herself at me, took me by surprise, gripped me with an incredible strength. "It's the same way with me," she panted. "I can't wait!"

The kitchen was the only place. But this time, it was different, without timidity and without restraint.

And when it was over, it was a gentle parting, reluctant yet peaceful and satisfying.

I lay on the floor, the hot, damp tiles feeling cool to my body, my head cradled in the hollow of her arm.

"Did you ever think it would be this way?" I asked.

"It never has been," she replied, and by the sudden tightening of her fingers, I knew she was thinking of Freidman, the way he brutally tortured her at night.

"How do you feel now? Doesn't the heat in this room kinda knock you out?"

"I'm used to it," she said. There was a pause. She added: "I feel kinda good now."

"You're not sorry ... about us, I mean?"

She ran her fingers through my hair, drew her fingernails down my cheek, traced a pattern on my chest. "Of course not," she whispered.

I could feel the sweat running down from my shoulders, trickling on to the floor. "This heat gets me," I gasped. "Kinda takes all the strength out of me."

She made a slight movement. "I'd better get dressed."

I held her tightly, restrainingly. "Just a few minutes more," I pleaded. "Just a few minutes more."

She relaxed. We were silent for a while, and then she said, quietly: "How are we going to do it? How are we going to get away from here?"

"I've been thinking," I told her. "We could go now if we wanted. The only thing we lack is dough. That, and clothes for you to wear. But I can get them somehow, and we'll go together."

She slewed around, half-sat, taking her weight on her arm. "Let's dress. We'll talk after."

"Just another minute."

"All right, honey," she whispered. She leaned over me, her hair brushing my face, her lips moist on mine, her belly slippery with sweat. Then, as her lips touched mine, it happened.

It was as unexpected as snow in the Sahara, and happened with the shocking explosion of an atom bomb. The kitchen window exploded inwards, glass spattering and falling like hail, splintered wood groaning as it splintered from the window frame and the bright sun slashing in at us like a search light.

Yeah, it was Freidman.

He had used a wooden chopping block to smash in that back door window, and he wasn't gonna need any explanations.

Both of us lying on the floor together, startled and panic-stricken, sprinkled with fragments of glass, were all the explanations he would ever need.

They woke me by smacking my face hard. It seemed as though I hadn't slept in weeks and they'd let me doze for just a minute.

81

I peered up into his face, greasy and glistening in the dull light of the cell.

"All right, Farran," he growled. "Let's go."

There wasn't one muscle that wasn't an unholy ache. I made an effort to prop myself up on my elbow, fell back with a groan.

"Let's go," he growled, irritably. "I ain't even begun to work on you yet."

Then there was somebody levering him to one side, standing over me, staring down at me calculatingly.

I stared up at him through the slits of my eyes. His uniform showed he was the cop captain.

He said, in a warning voice: " You mustn't overdo it. He looks pretty bad."

"Resisted arrest," grunted the fat dick. "A guy always gets banged about when he resists arrest."

The cop captain said, through his teeth: "He deserves it, the little bastard. But be smart. Don't get the Department in trouble. Give him a chance to get his strength back. Right now he looks bad. Ya gotta be careful with a guy like this. His nerve might go. His brain might even crack."

The fat guy said: "We ain't got much time to work him over. We'll have to hand him over to the State soon."

"Give him another hour," said the cop captain.

The fat dick sighed. "Frying's too good for this guy. The State will be far too easy with him."

There was a long silence. The cop captain said, bitterly: "I've got two kids just the same age as those he murdered. If it had happened to my own two kids, I couldn't feel any meaner."

The fat dick said: "The law don't always fit the angles. The most the law can do is execute him. But we've got a duty, too. We've got to even up the best we can, make him suffer, even if it has to be unofficial."

The cop captain warned: "Lay off him for another half-an-hour, then."

I watched them go out, found myself cringing from the loathing and contempt in their voices.

"Those two kids he murdered," the cop captain had said.

Those two kids I murdered!

Two kids ... I murdered!

CHAPTER NINE

It was just by chance I met Johnny Miller and Harry Stokes. I was standing on the corner debating if I should go to the movies or go back home for my swimming costume when their car drew into the kerb beside me with a loud squeal of tyres.

"What ya doing?" called Johnny.

"Nothing special," I told him.

He indicated the back seat. "Climb in."

The car was Johnny's father's, a Hudson convertible, new, as fresh and as clean and flashy as an ornament on a Christmas tree.

He drew away from the kerb and out into the traffic with a jerk that showed he didn't know how to use the gears properly. I leaned forward from the back seat, said into his ear: "Your pa know you've got his car?"

"Sure," said Johnny, without assurance.

"His folks have gone visiting," explained Harry. "Won't be back until tomorrow."

Then me and Harry kinda clung on tight while Johnny built up speed, cut in and out of the traffic.

"Where are we going?" I asked after a pause, the wind ruffling up my hair and making it difficult for me to breathe.

"Just a run-around," he said with a grin, and I just caught the sly wink he threw at Harry.

We drove around for a while, then just as I was wishing I'd gone to the movies instead, Johnny pulled into the kerb, climbed out from behind the steering wheel.

"Take her over, Farran," he said. "Test her out. See how you like her style."

I forgot all about the movies. The chance to drive a new, sleek job like this was far too good an opportunity. I didn't worry I hadn't a driving licence, or that my driving had hitherto been subjected to supervision.

Johnny took my seat in the back, I got down behind the steering wheel and got going.

I cruised up and down getting the feel of the car first, the way she reacted to the wheel and the engine revs as I passed through the gears. When I had the feel of her, I began to head out of town.

Johnny said casually, so casually I knew right away the whole thing was a fix: "Just drift along around Tree Street, Farran. There's a coupla friends we might pick up."

It didn't worry me. I had the feel of that car now, and it could do speed. I was anxious and aching to get her on the open road.

I doubled back, cruised along Tree Street, pulled into the kerb opposite two dames who were waiting there.

I didn't know them, hadn't seen them before. They were maybe eighteen or nineteen. Nobody bothered to introduce me, and one squeezed in front between me and Harry and the other climbed in back alongside Johnny.

"Okay, Farran," said Johnny. "All set now. Let's make for the wide-open spaces."

I threaded my way out on to the main drag, rammed my foot down, felt a thrill inside me as the car responded immediately.

There were giggles coming from the back of the car. Harry and the dame alongside me were so close it looked like it was gonna need a crowbar to pry them apart.

I wasn't so dumb I didn't realise I'd been invited along so the boys could have their hands free.

But I wasn't worrying one little bit. I had no kicks about playing chauffeur. I'd rather have had that car throbbing under my fingertips than either of the two dames.

That car was a dream. I didn't take any risks with it, but every time there was an opportunity, I jacked it up as high as it would go, kept it flat out as long as traffic permitted.

Johnny said: "There's a little place over the next hill where we can dance."

Harry said: "That's it, Farran. Pull in there."

It was getting dark as I crested the hill, glided down the other side and pulled into the car park alongside a long, timber-built shack laced with fairy lights.

84

I put on the brake, turned off the engine and started to climb out of the car.

"That's right, Farran," said Johnny. "You go right on inside. We'll join you in a few minutes."

The girl who was with him giggled.

Harry came out of his clinch long enough to say: "That's right, Farran. We won't keep you long."

I shrugged, turned off the car lights, climbed out of the car door. Just a coupla paces away, they were indistinct shadows in the dusk.

I went inside, bought myself a beer, carried it over to a table. There were one or two fellas dancing with their dolls. A mournful jukebox wailed a slow, tentative blues, and the bartender rested his elbows on the counter, gazed sadly into the past.

Almost an hour passed before I decided to go look for them, and as I got up from the table, they came in.

Harry's usually carefully-smarmed hair was standing up in spikes; Johnny's face was flushed, and he looked uncomfortable. The two dames were quiet, had got over their giggling mood and had applied fresh make-up in the car. They'd put it on too thick. In the glare of the naked roof lights, they managed to look like cheap prostitutes.

They sat at my table, and nobody seemed to want to say anything. The bartender came over, wiped down the table with a damp cloth, looked at us enquiringly.

"Four beers," said Johnny.

"How about a chaser?" said Harry.

Johnny looked at the dames, raised one eyebrow enquiringly.

"I don't mind," said one dully.

"Just as you like," said the other.

"Four ryes to follow," Johnny told the bartender.

"I'll have another beer," I told the bartender.

All the zest had gone out of the party, a party finished long before it was due to finish.

Harry swallowed his beer at one draught, tossed his rye straight down on top of it.

The two girls sipped their beers, watched Johnny dawdle with his glass and stare into it moodily.

Harry said, abruptly: "This is a hell of a party. Let's snap it up." He climbed to his feet, reached for the hand of one of the dames – Johnny's dame!

It didn't give Johnny any alternative but to take the dame Harry had been wrestling with.

That kinda revived interest for all four of them. They came back to the table and changed partners permanently, Harry and Johnny sitting with their arms around the girls' waists and the girls happy and simpering coyly. Johnny ordered a second round of beers and chasers. I didn't want to drink, on account I was driving, but didn't want to appear a milksop. Maybe the beer alone wouldn't have been so bad, but the chaser was kinda warming. Not that it got me pickled; or even happy. I had a warm glow inside me that made me feel good. I danced with Johnny's dame, but I wasn't so happy about that. She had a way of dancing that made it seem she was lying on me, moving her legs only when mine moved them for her. She kept giggling, nudging my chest with hers, and all the time Johnny was sitting there, scowling heavily.

I was glad to get back to the table.

Johnny ordered more drinks. I managed to duck out of mine, switched my rye glass when Harry had emptied his. The beer had a kinda warm, flat taste, like the bartender figured we wouldn't now know the difference.

Harry said: "Let's get out of here. It's too crowded."

His dame giggled, and she swayed as she climbed to her feet. He had to put his arms around her to steady her. She clutched him tightly, closed her eyes like she was going to sleep standing up.

"You carry on," said Johnny. "I'll settle the bill."

"I'll take care of it," said Harry.

Johnny slipped him a sly wink. "Leave it with me," he said.

Harry took both girls' arms, and we went back to the car, climbed inside; me behind the steering wheel with Johnny's girl next to me. Her hands were hot and moist, and she edged up against me, rested her head on my shoulder.

I eased her away from me when I saw Johnny coming. She sneered, unsteadily: "What's the matter, honey? Don't you like me?"

Johnny heard that. His eyes became black and sullen. He glared at me. "What goes on, Farran," he demanded, wanting trouble.

I sighed. "Don't be stupid. The dame's half-cut. She's got the giggles, needs looking after."

"I'll look after her if she needs it."

"That's what I mean," I told him. "Where were you?"

He opened the door of the car, and for the first time I saw the package under his arm. He climbed inside, rested the packet on the floor beside him, slammed the door and reached out for the girl. She went eagerly, smoothly and willingly, like a seal sliding into the water. I saw his hand go under her armpit and half around front of her, and heard her little, half-tipsy mew of pleasure.

"Let's get going, Farran," Johnny said. "You concentrate on driving. We're gonna be kinda busy." His voice was thick and his words slurred. He'd drunk just about as much as he could take.

I switched on the headlights, thumbed the engine into life and glided out on to the main drag. We'd covered plenty of road, and it was a long drive back to town. I was looking forward to it. The road was clear of traffic now. I wanted to feel the surge of power when I got that speedometer hitting the top peg. I wanted to feel wind in my hair, hear the whine of the tyres, and intoxicate myself with the pure thrill of speed.

Johnny's dame whispered something urgently.

"What's that?" he demanded. "What say?"

"Button," she complained more loudly. "It's come off."

"We'll find it later," he growled.

By sitting up very straight, I could just see the reflection in the driving mirror of Harry and the other dame in the back seat. They were blurred, indistinct shadows, suspiciously quiet.

The dame beside me, suddenly anxious, said: "No, Johnny. Not that!"

"I know what you need," he said, thickly. "You need another drink." He reached down beside him, and I heard the rustle of brown paper. I knew he had bought a bottle of rye.

I kept on driving, dimming my headlights for approaching cars, finding the other headlights were blinding me, hurting my eyes.

She said: "I don't want any, Johnny."

"Drink it," he ordered. "Straight from the bottle. It'll make you feel good."

"But I don't ..."

"Sure you do," he insisted.

She pretended to take a sip, handed the bottle back to him.

He tilted back his head, and I knew he was overdoing it. You can't drink rye straight from the bottle like that. It turns your stomach, goes to your head, makes you feel like hell the next day.

"Drink some more," he instructed.

"No, Johnny," she said. "I don't want ..."

I shot him a quick glance. He had his arm around her neck, was locking her head. She was struggling with him as he tilted the bottle against her lips. She musta drank some of it, because she coughed and spluttered, some of it trickling from her chin, dripping down the front of her dress that gaped open.

"Makes you feel good," he insisted. "Takes away the cobwebs." He raised the bottle to his own lips, tilted his head back.

I was beginning to build up speed now. The oncoming traffic was less, and the glare of the headlights wasn't hurting my eyes so much. The engine was a quiet purr, the tyres hummed softly, and the wind was sharp against my cheek.

She gave a pained kinda whisper. "No, Johnny. Not that. Not that!"

"What you need is another drink," he growled.

There was an open stretch on the road, with nothing head of me as far as I could see. I rammed my foot down hard.

"Quit it, Johnny. You're hurting!"

"Take another little drink," he said.

I could feel the car lifting, kinda soaring beneath me as I gave her the gun, on the point of leaving the ground.

She was struggling with him now. He had one hand clamped round her neck, his other forcing the bottle against her lips.

The road was a narrow, white ribbon streaming to a pinpoint. The roadside trees formed a tunnel through which we hurtled at awe-inspiring speed, and the steering wheel was trembling a little, our speed just a little too high for safety.

They were struggling in earnest now, both of them sliding over against me, her shoulder jamming against mine, as she tried to twist her mouth away from the bottle.

"Don't, Johnny," she pleaded desperately. "Don't. It'll go all over me."

"Do what I say," he ordered, harshly. "You've got to loosen up, get some of the starch out of you."

"I won't, Johnny. I won't. I'll scream!"

There was a bend far ahead, headlights sweeping around it, indicating a car approaching in the opposite direction.

Johnny was ramming hard against me, twisting around in his seat so he was straddling across her. He'd got one hand locked in her hair, dragging her head back, and she'd got both hands clamped around his wrist, struggling to prevent him from forcing the bottle towards her mouth.

"Cut it out, you two," I yelled. "What do you wanna do? Cause an accident?"

I was swinging into the bend now, and was gonna meet the other car right on the bend. His headlights were powerful. I braced myself, humped my shoulders against the dame, leaned heavily on the wheel and fed the car into the bend.

"You'll drink when I tell you," snarled Johnny, and he jerked his bottle hand free from her grasp.

It was rye, strong rye. The raw liquor spurted from the bottle, splashed into my face, trickled down over my chin. The sting of it was molten fire in my eyes, mingled with the slashing glare of the approaching headlights. I couldn't see. The hot sting of my eyes was blinding me, driving me crazy. In a kinda frantic desperation, I knew I must hang on to the steering wheel, coax the car around that curve. Because to apply brakes at that moment would put me into a skid I couldn't pull out of, that would wrap the car around a tree.

89

Everything was happening instantaneously, the splash of burning rye in my eyes, the slash of headlights, and the vague shimmer of the road ahead – all I could see of it through my smarting eyes.

The other car missed us by inches. I'd miscalculated, drawn too far over on the far side of the road. I managed to correct in time, pulled hard on the wheel, got into a counter swerve that needed all my strength to keep us on the road.

And then it happened; that unexpected, awful, dreadful thing that tortured me day and night.

And it happened in slow motion; the blurred slice of road shimmering ahead of me, the swerving arc as our car plunged towards the side of the road, and then, in my path, the two blurred figures walking side by side.

There was no time, no hope of avoiding them. Sickeningly I tried, wrenched hard on the wheel as they seemed to be flung at me. The car swerved crazily as sound echoed through it from the impact on the wings and radiator. I was half-frozen with shock, feeling the back wheels bump up and over something while at the same time the trees on the opposite side of the road screamed towards me.

My hands were frozen to the steering wheel, and I was limp inside. The brake pedal was flat to the floor, the tyres screaming. I thought I wasn't going to make it, thought the car would bury itself up to its back axle in a tree. And it was all happening in slow motion; the steering wheel of the car pulling around slowly, the wheels bumping up on the grass verge, trees slewing around in front of the bonnet, scraping along the side of the car.

The tyres were still screeching, the steering wheel slippery in my sweating hands as I fought to pull out of the speed wobble. Inside of me was the terrible fear for the awful thing that had happened, the dreadful, ghastly sound as wings and bonnet pulped human flesh, the bump of the back wheels vibrating right up through the steering wheel.

The car was steady now, slowing down, almost at a standstill. Johnny was reaching across the dame, gouging his fingers into my shoulder, shaking me hard. "Don't stop," he was yelling. "For heaven's sake, keep going. Keep driving."

His dame was sobbing hysterically, and the smell of whisky was strong in my nostrils. My clothes were soaked in it, and broken glass scrunched beneath our feet.

Johnny was punching at my shoulder, his voice frantic. "Keep driving, you damned fool. Keep driving."

I couldn't think clearly, and a dreadful, frightened numbness had overtaken me, through which Johnny's frantic voice penetrated, urging again and again, "Keep driving. Don't stop."

I stamped my foot down on the gas, automatically worked my way up through the gears. The dame was still sobbing, Johnny was sitting hunched up, cold sober, and I was ice-cold, without feeling.

Johnny said, in a kinda choked voice: "Take this second-class road along here. Get on to the side roads, keep driving as hard as you can."

I obeyed automatically. I couldn't feel anything at all now, but I knew pretty soon it was gonna hit me with bang.

"It wasn't your fault," said Johnny, hoarsely. "The other guy's headlights blinded you."

"That rye," I said, tonelessly. "It splashed in my face, blinded me."

He said in a small, tight voice: "You've got to keep quiet about the whisky. There wasn't any in the car. Understand? I never took the car out. Understand? If my pop learns I've been out in his car, drinking with a coupla dames, he'll half kill me. So keep your trap shut."

"They'll want to know everything," I said dully, after I turned into a narrow secondary road.

"They ain't even gonna know we did it," he said, hoarsely. "None of us is gonna talk. Get it? We didn't drive anywhere near here. We weren't in this neck of the woods. We're all gonna pull together, tell the same story."

Harry said from the back of the car, in an awed and frightened voice: "Any damage to the car?"

"Pull over to the side," Johnny instructed. "We'll give it the once-over."

I pulled into the side of the road, put on the brakes. I noticed for the first time that I was sweating, my clothes damp and my face glistening.

91

Johnny dug down in the dashboard locker, came up with a flash lamp. "If it's just a bent fender," he said, "we can straighten it out, put the car back in the garage without pop knowing about it."

I went around front with him, stared for a few seconds at the front of the car, not quite understanding. Then, when I did, I was violently sick.

The car had a mouth-organ bonnet. The wings were dented and there were splashes of blood on the front of the car. Worst of all was the white, blood-flecked something still mashed in the radiator.

Harry made the two girls stay in the car, came around front and joined us. He said slowly, white-faced, "We're not going to get away with this, Farran. We should have stopped back there. They're gonna send out a police call, and every car that goes in for repairs is gonna be checked."

Johnny said, quickly: "I've got to stop my old man from knowing."

"You can't stop him," said Harry, bluntly. "It'll all have to come out. Anyway, what are you worried about? You weren't driving."

Johnny said, agitatedly: "My father will kill me. It makes it worse letting Farran drive."

"You've got to wise up," snarled Harry. "Within an hour, every cop car in town is gonna be searching for a hit-and-run driver. We're not gonna get away with this, none of us. The best thing is head right back to town and turn ourselves in."

"That's fine for you," sneered Johnny. "You ain't got nothing to worry about."

"So that makes it fine for me. And it makes me objective. I can see both angles. And I'm giving you valuable advice."

My hands were shaking. I said: "Look, fellas. There's another angle. We could leave the car here, just the way it is. It could have been stolen. Anyone could have taken it up from the kerbside and driven off with it. How does that sound?"

"That's lousy," said Harry. "We've got to get back to town, park these two dames and forget we ever saw them. Then we've got to go straight to police headquarters."

Johnny sighed. "I guess we've got to do just that," he agreed, reluctantly. "Okay, Farran, let's go."

I was sweating again, my hands and knees were trembling. I was in no state to drive.

"Listen, fellas," I said, and my teeth were chattering. "One of you fellas had better drive it in."

They went so rigid I could almost feel the suspicion emanating from them.

"Are you crazy?" demanded Harry.

"What are you trying to swing?" rasped Johnny.

"Look at my hands," I pleaded, almost crying. "I'm all shot. I can't drive like this."

Harry said softly, menacingly: "You'll drive, Farran. You can't swing this on to us. You'll drive. Even at five miles an hour!" A warning note came into his voice. "Don't forget, Farran. We can help you. We were witnesses. But just don't try and cross us up."

I got down behind the steering wheel, eased her along at maybe ten miles an hour. Nobody said anything. There was a kinda grim, dread silence. My numbed mind was working now, slowly, but with a kinda ruthless analysis.

I could see the way it was. A hit-and-run driver, whisky-soaked upholstery, whisky on my clothing, alcohol in my blood that would respond to a medical test.

Additionally, the car wasn't mine. I hadn't a driving licence, I wasn't insured and there was no chance I could plead I hadn't known I'd knocked them down.

There was still that grisly, blood-smeared fragment hanging from the radiator!

I felt faint, wanted to be sick again. I was thinking what it must be like back there. An ambulance, police cars, and their headlights throwing a pale, merciless light on the grisly scene.

I was young and had all my life before me. Maybe I would get five years, maybe ten years. I might even get life on a homicide charge.

I'd been drinking. All of us had been drinking. That was the biggest crime of all.

We were getting near town now, and there was a dread, cold chill in the pit of my belly, because I was alone. None of them was gonna help me. They were out to save their own skins. Right deep down inside me, I knew Johnny was never gonna admit struggling with the dame or splashing whisky in my face.

I passed a small bar set back from the road, and at the same time felt a wave of greyness sweep up and over me.

I managed to pull into the road and apply the brakes before I kinda collapsed, sat there with my head in my hands, eyes closed, trying to shake off the sickness.

Johnny shone his flashlamp in my face. "Don't go chicken, Farran," he gritted. "You've got to go through with it. We've all got to go through with it."

"I'll be all right in a minute," I gasped, weakly.

"Sure," he said. "We'll go straight to town, straight to police headquarters, tell them exactly how it happened."

"I feel bad," I mumbled.

Harry said suddenly, solicitously: "How about a bracer, Farran. Just a snorter to put your nerves right."

I shuddered, squared my shoulders.

"Yeah, that's an idea," said Johnny. "There's a bar not far back down the road. Get yourself a bracer. It's what you need."

It was so obvious they were wanting me smelling of drink, it made me ashamed for them.

Yet it didn't make any difference. The alcohol was already in my blood. The police tests would bring it out. And I did badly need a bracer.

"We'll wait here for you," said Johnny, encouragingly.

Wordlessly, unsteadily, I climbed out from the car, walked back the fifty yards or so to the bar.

It was deserted except for a truck driver who was sipping a soft drink. I guess I musta appeared bad, because he gave me a strange look when he saw me.

I went over to the counter, held on tightly to it, amazed at the hardness of the wood beneath my fingers. I ordered a rye.

The bartender poured slowly, watched me with one eye. "Looks like you can do with it, son," he commented.

I said nothing, gave him the money and took my change.

94

The truck driver nodded to the bartender, went outside.

I clutched the glass firmly in my hand, knew I'd have to drink it all down in one go. If I tried sipping it, I'd gag, vomit it over the counter.

The radio crackled, and the Melody Players were abruptly switched off the air.

The announcer said:

"News flash. All car drivers and garages in this vicinity are asked to be on the look-out for a hit-and-run convertible. It is almost certain the car will have damage to wings and fenders. The police should be informed immediately if ..."

I was numb inside. I didn't think my face reflected any emotion. But the bartender was staring at me strangely.

I could see the way it was gonna be. Even before I turned myself in, they'd capture me. I wasn't gonna have a chance to go in clean.

It meant maybe ten or fifteen years in jail.

It could even mean life!

And I was just twenty.

I downed the rye in one gulp, slid the glass back on the counter, took a grip on myself, turned around and walked steadily towards the door.

Just outside, the red rear lights of the truck driver's wagon pierced the darkness. I could see the rear lights of the Ford convertible parked up the road, the four of them waiting for me to come back and drive them into town.

And suddenly I knew fear. Blind, unreasoning fear. I saw the hand of the law stretching out to engulf me, crush me, imprison me for a life-time.

It was all so easy and so natural. The truck driver slammed into gear, stamped on the gas. The truck ground into movement, tyres grinding on the gravel. The tail of the truck swung past me with hitch ropes hanging, almost falling into my hands.

It was like the gods had dropped a solution in my lap.

A few minutes later, clinging to the swaying tailboard of the truck, I could no longer see the tail-lights of convertible. Rapidly I was leaving it further and further behind me.

95

They changed their tactics. They removed the irons from my wrists and ankles, and seated me in a heavy oak chair with my wrists and ankles pinioned by biting leather straps.

I'd been sitting in that chair under that fierce white light for weeks. Maybe it was years.

Since I'd been in their hands, I hadn't eaten. But that didn't worry me. My body was numbed with pain, and the pangs of hunger hardly affected me.

But I hadn't drunk either, and thirst was driving me mad. My throat, mouth and tongue rasped together like sandpaper.

The fat dick's bulk blocked out the glare of the arc light. It blazed down at me savagely. He rasped, viciously: " You're getting the idea now, kid. Just so long as we can give it to you, you're gonna take it. We can pay you back in a way the law can't. Just tell us how you like it, killer. Come on. Speak up. How d'you like it?"

I didn't say anything, couldn't say anything. My tongue was swollen, clogging my mouth. I closed my eyes, let feeling drain down to my boots, and waited for it.

It came. His palm against my cheek, slapping my head sideways, even rocking the heavy oak chair.

"How d'you like it?" he insisted.

I tried to say something, tried to plead with him. But my swollen tongue and sandpaper mouth could only make uncouth noises.

The fat guy switched on a tone of sympathy. " Well, what d'ya know, he's thirsty. He needs a drink. Get him a drink, boys."

I'd been through the routine twice before. I writhed back in my chair, arms straining at the unbreakable leather straps. One of them looped his arm around my neck, forcing my head back and holding it immovable. The other held my nose, pried my teeth apart with a wedge of wood that kept my jaws apart while the fat guy poured.

Poured is the wrong word. It was a tumbler of mustard and salt whipped up to a treacle-like consistency. And so I shouldn't spit it out, they rammed it home with a ball of cotton wool, secured it firmly between my jaws with a neck-tie.

My mouth, tongue and head were on fire. I couldn't breathe. My eyes were staring from my head, spurting tears, *and sulphur fumes were up around back of my nose, choking and suffocating like poison gas.*

"Makes you think of Freidman, doesn't it, killer?" he gloated.

I was dying.

This time, I was dying for sure. Trying to breathe meant inhaling liquid fire that was splitting my chest apart, boiling my brain and incinerating my thoughts.

"It sure makes you think of Freidman!" he gloated.

CHAPTER TEN

Freidman.

Freidman!

FREIDMAN.

The shattering impact of wood against glass was numbing, paralysing.

I sat up, stared at him wide-eyed, my heart beating madly but my brain numb, dead, refusing to function.

She was sitting beside me, eyes staring, her face white. I could hear her gasping like she was sucking in breath but wasn't exhaling.

Freidman's head and shoulders framed in the smashed window frame looked enormous, his eyes, black and vindictive, smiling with an evil menace. But his voice was quiet, quieter than I'd ever heard it before, almost a purr.

He said, softly: "Come over and open this door."

She was trembling, her body trying to obey, but fear paralysing her.

"Open this door," he said again, and the note of command in his voice was urgent now, imperative.

I could feel her body throbbing and vibrating, as her muscles went into action.

"Hurry," he said through his teeth.

She got to her feet, slowly, reluctantly. I wanted to stop her, grasp her by the wrist, prevent her from unlocking the door that was the only barrier between him and us.

But my bones were like jelly, my brain a vacuum, unable to communicate instructions to my body.

In a kinda dream, I saw her crossing to the door, her white haunches quivering, her bare feet treading down the shafts of glass seemingly without feeling, blood spurting, staining the stone floor.

A strangled protest tore free from inside me. I said hoarsely, in a voice that wasn't mine: "No, don't go. Don't let him in."

She was a robot, frightened and numbed, obeying the voice of a man she feared. She turned the key in the lock, and then Freidman was turning the door handle, thrusting the door back with such force that it sent her staggering backwards, her shoulders hitting the wall.

There was almost malicious satisfaction in his eyes as he closed the door behind him, turned the key in the lock and put the key in his pocket.

I felt the strength slowly creeping back to my limbs. I crouched, got ready to climb to my feet.

He said, with a dreadful note in his voice: "Just as I thought."

She was staring at him terror-stricken, her hands crossed against her naked breasts.

I was wondering if a flying leap would enable me to reach the kitchen door, so I could bolt through it into the dining room.

But he was thinking way ahead of me, his reflexes working rapidly. He circled around me quickly, got between me and the dining room door, bolted it securely.

I didn't climb to my feet. I continued to crouch like I was getting ready to run a race. I was trembling with fear. He walked across to me slowly, his thin lips twisted in a malicious grin of pleasure. "I like you better standing, son," he gritted, and his fingers locked in my hair, dragged me to my feet.

I hadn't any complaints. I deserved it, and I got it. His knotted fist uppercutted, scrunched against my jaw, lifted me off my feet, smashed me backwards so my shoulders hit the stone floor and I skidded until my head hit the wall.

In a grey mist of pain, I sat up, shook my head. My mouth was full of blood and my head was bleeding. Then, with a coward's relief, I saw that he had left me, had turned his attention to his wife.

"Come here," he said.

She came. Slowly, unwillingly, terror-stricken.

But she came!

He locked his fingers in her hair, grinned sadistically. "You decided to play, huh? You betrayed your husband, who's been good to you. Taken on the first little whelp who's come along. And you thought I was stupid, didn't you? Thought I didn't realise what was going on. You're just a no-good bitch, aren't you?"

Her eyes were glazed with terror, her knees trembling, but her hands were passive at her sides.

"You're a no-good bitch," he said.

With her hair coiled around his hand, he kinda strained her on tip-toe while he smacked her face from side to side maybe half-a-dozen times. He wasn't playing. Her lips spurted blood and her eyes became glazed. Yet she made no atempt to avoid the blows, just kinda hung by her hair unprotestingly, arms at her sides.

"You're a no-good bitch," he snarled.

She didn't even whimper, merely half-closed her eyes in pain.

"Say it," he snarled. "You're a no-good bitch. Say it!"

"I'm a no-good bitch," she mumbled, through split lips.

"I'm gonna teach you a lesson," he grated. "I'm gonna teach you both a lesson you'll never forget. I'm gonna teach you to be sorry for the day you took your husband for a sucker."

The numbness was leaving my jaw now, replaced by the beginning of pain. The haziness was evaporating too, everything taking on a clear-cut outline.

Freidman hooked a chair over to him with his foot, sat down on it, tugged viciously on her hair to make her kneel at his feet.

"I'm gonna teach you," he snarled. "I'm gonna learn both of you. You're gonna have a lesson you'll never forget. A permanent reminder that you won't be able to stop thinking about, the next time you start tom-catting."

I wiped the blood away from my mouth, sat up, looked calculatingly at the dining room door. There was just a chance that I could get away, if only she would struggle with him, distract his attention.

He repeated slowly, maliciously: "A lesson you'll never forget." He fumbled in his pocket, produced a jack-knife, flicked it with his thumb so that the short, sharp blade glistened in the sun streaming through the broken window.

I was more scared now. She was a dame as well as his wife, and there wasn't much pain he could inflict on her that she hadn't already received. Even if he did cut off her hair, it would grow again. She was in the kitchen all the time anyway, so she didn't have to worry about her appearance.

But I wasn't his wife. He could get real mean with me, maybe carve me up a little with that knife. The fear was deep down in the pit of my belly, growing stronger and wilder every moment, making me frantic so that I was calculating the chances of a headlong dive through the broken window.

He snarled, "Come here, you trollop," and jerked savagely on her hair, toppling her over on top of him so that she sprawled across his knees, face uppermost.

There was wild fear inside me as I stared in amazement, watched his arm clamp across her belly so that she writhed, her head hanging, almost touching the stone floor.

Then he raised the knife, held her in such a way that both she and I understood in the same dreadful moment the horrible, unbelievable intention in his mind.

She screamed, a wild, frantic scream that came from a tormented brain. And the fantastically brutal vengeance he was planning, killed my fear, made me frantic to stop him at all costs.

He saw me coming, was probably expecting me to attack. I was like a crazy thing, while he was quite cool and detached. As my arm crooked around his neck, he smashed his knife hand at me; not the blade, but the butt of his hand from which protruded the haft of the knife. It was a huge hand, and he used all his strength. I knew only that the front of my face had been staved in, that I was flying, that my shoulders smashed against hard substance, that I was lying on the floor, arched in pain and the grey mist enveloping me again.

Then, through the grey mist, I heard her tortured scream, knew that he meant to do this terrible thing, knew that although it was against every instinct of man, he would also do it to me. Cold fear combined with my desperate, outraged horror gave me a strength and a fearlessness that was not a part of me.

The grey haze was edging close around me as I staggered to my feet, lurched unsteadily towards him.

She was screaming, shriek after shriek, terrible, tormenting screams that speared down deep into the depths of my soul. I knew I had to stop him, stop this dreadful thing he was doing, stop him somehow although his strength was ten times mine.

The black mist edging in on me flickered, and momentarily I saw a means by which I could prevent this terrible mutilation. I saw the flat iron she used for tea-cloths, innocent and domestic-looking but a powerful weapon.

I waded through the black mist and her shrill, terrifying screams. I saw the flat iron awaiting my hand, felt it weighing down my arm. I saw the flicker of his knife and heard just one more desperate, soul-crazed scream while my arm was lifting, moving.

He began to turn, to swing his knife arm up to take the force of my blow, and I saw his eyes then, glowing and crazed, froth bubbling at the corners of his mouth. I knew then there was nothing that would stop him, nothing that could restrain his brute strength and crazed purpose.

He howled like an agonised wolf as the iron smashed his arm. But in the same moment, he thrust her from his lap, switched the knife to his other hand, and then the leaping fear inside me took control so that, with frantic terror I swung again, smashed at his head, felt the impact shock me to the elbow. I shuddered with relief when he gave a kinda grunt, slumped slowly sideways, toppled to the floor.

I stood there for long seconds, my eyes closed, sweat streaming down me. I was trembling all over, like a nervous horse. My fingers unlocked nervelessly, and the flat iron fell to the floor.

I tried to fight feeling faint, walked over to her, knelt down beside her. She was doubled up, clutching herself. There was a streak of blood on the back of her hand.

I said, in a harsh, choked voice: "He didn't ...?"

"No ..." she panted. "It's just a cut."

I got to my feet unsteadily, went over to the sink, drew a pitcher of water from the tank. I poured it over myself, let the cold shock of it edge away that blackness, wash the blood from my face. I filled the pitcher again, went across to her. She was sitting up now, gazing at Freidman with terrified eyes.

I said, tersely: "We've got to leave now. We've got to go quick. We've got to get out of here before he comes round, before he kills us both."

She didn't answer. Just stared at Freidman,
I up-ended the jug over her.

It hadn't the slightest effect. I shook her by the shoulders. "We've got to get out of here," I urged. "Can't you understand what I'm telling you? He'll kill us."

She said, in a choked voice: "What did you do to him? What was it you did?"

Something in her voice startled me. I looked around at Freidman, felt the same, dread feeling that gripped her.

He was lying awkwardly on his side, his legs doubled up like he was still sitting. His jaw hung open and his eyes were staring.

Suddenly I wasn't breathing any more.

This wasn't happening to me. This wasn't real. It was happening to somebody else. I went over to him almost on tip-toe, stared down at him.

He still didn't look any different. I bent over him, noticed the trickle of blood crawling across his forehead and down into his ear.

His eyes were open and glazed, his mouth sagging like the neck muscles were broken.

I touched him.

It wasn't me living all this. It was someone else. It couldn't be me!

I bent down and fumbled for his pulse, couldn't find the right spot. And then I suddenly understood that nobody was ever gonna find his pulse again.

She said over my shoulder, in a scared voice: "My God. You've murdered him!"

CHAPTER ELEVEN

If you live with a thing long enough, you finally grow to accept it. But right then, it only vaguely registered on my consciousness that Freidman was dead.

I had killed him.

"What are we going to do?" she panted.

Escape!

That was the way my mind was learning to work. Escape! It was so much easier to run than stay and face the consequences.

"We've got to get away from here," I panted. "But it looks bad. Nobody will believe it was an accident. There was that trucker who saw us the other day. He'll say it was planned!"

I wasn't only escaping from Freidman. I was wanting to escape from those two figures searchlighted in my headlights, being flung against the bonnet of my car with sickening impact.

"Where will we go?" she asked, scared. "What will we do?"

"We've got to get out of here first," I panted. "Get away from here. We'll decide what to do later."

She looked down at Freidman, and her face was expressionless. "You had to kill him," she said quietly. "There wasn't any other way of stopping him."

I was sweating, but my sweat was ice-cold. "You're in this with me," I told her thickly. "You've got to help me. Understand? You've got to help me."

She looked up at me anxiously. "I'll do anything. Anything you say." She shuddered. "I never knew people died so easily."

I raised my arm, wiped the sweat off my brow. It was almost a surprise to find that my mind was working smoothly, efficiently, weighing all the angles, deciding my line of action.

I bent over him, went through his pockets. It gave me goose-pimples to touch him, because he was strangely cold and his glazed eyes were staring over my head as though he could see the future. Yet I had to do it. I straightened up holding the key of the bedroom, the car key, a slim leather wallet containing a few bucks, and his watch.

She said, in a whisper: "What do you want me to do?"

"Get dressed," I told her, curtly.

We both dressed, and when putting on my shoes, I noticed for the first time that my feet too were cut by the broken glass. And I hadn't even known about it!

"Haven't you got any shoes at all?" I asked. "Aren't there any in the bedroom?"

She shook her head dully. "Not a thing. Not a thing to wear apart from this dress."

That made me feel better. It brought back unpleasant memories of Freidman, his sadism, his grim enjoyment of her suffering; the way he had turned her into a slave, enduring subtle tortures, and the way he had slowly been increasing his hold over me.

It didn't seem then such a terrible thing to have killed him.

She asked, in a quavering voice: "What will they do if they catch us?"

I didn't even want to think about being caught. In the same way that my body was escaping, my mind was escaping too. I was telling myself that this was all a dream, that it hadn't really happened, that tomorrow I would awaken and everything would be all right.

I had indeed almost convinced myself it was a dream. I said: "We can't leave him around where any casual caller is likely to see him. Understand?"

She stared at me, wide-eyed. "What will we do with ..." She broke off, suddenly understanding.

"If the worse comes to the worse, that's the way it happened," I told her. "An accident. You understand?"

She nodded dumbly, grim realisation making her pale.

"Wait here," I instructed.

I propped the kitchen door open with a rock, went around front of the shack, looked along the road both directions. As far as I could see, there wasn't a car in sight.

The sun was beginning to go down now. What had to be done, could be done better while there was light.

I went back to the kitchen, and she was waiting quietly and obediently, with almost the same attitude she adopted towards Freidman. "We'll do it now," I told her. "Do it quick and get it over."

I expected her to be jumpy and nervous, shuddering at the touch of him. But she stared down at him impassively, as though he was no more than a sack of coals.

We each took an arm, dragged him between us. His weight was unbelievable. At first I thought we'd never shift him. Then, when he did move, the heels of his thick boots scuffed across the stone floor with a noise like a knife on an enamel plate.

We paused at the kitchen door, took a breather before we dragged him down the steps. His head cracked against each step, rolled from side to side, his jaw sagging open, like he was about to make a great shout of protest.

Now we'd got him moving, we kept at it, kept dragging him across the sun-dried earth, his trailing boot-heels leaving two wavy, irregular grooves.

We were panting badly by the time we got him to the well. We were out in the open now, could be easily seen by anyone passing. It wasn't the time to take a rest. We lifted him between us. Edging his head and shoulders over the lip of the well was the most difficult thing. It took us all of five minutes.

We had to stop and rest. He was half over the well parapet, his arms, head and shoulders dangling, almost blocking the narrow well.

I wiped my forearm across my forehead, looked at her meaningfully. "Ready?"

Her breasts were heaving, sweat running down her forehead. She nodded wordlessly.

I bent down, took a grip on his knees. She bent even lower, clasped her hands around his ankles.

I nodded at her, and simultaneously we straightened up. He was like a see-saw. As soon as we lifted his legs high enough, the weight of his body was pulling him down.

"Okay," I choked. "Let go."

Something caught, maybe it was his belt. He kinda hung there, half in the well and half out, but not falling. I gave him a push, a tiny push. Then his legs kinda slithered out of sight, disappeared over the lip of the well with the smooth, silent ease of a seal taking to water.

Those few seconds of waiting seemed like an eternity. It seemed we were waiting, waiting, waiting, for hours while he made that final, headlong dive. Fear jagged through me. I imagined the walls of the well narrowing, his huge bulk jammed between them, unmoving. Then, as fear caught at my throat, choking me, we heard it; heard the splash!

It was a faint splash, a long way away, deep down in the bowels of the earth. I hung over the lip of the well, tried to see to the bottom. But the sun was setting fast and I could see nothing but blackness.

I went back to the kitchen, got the torch that hung on the wall, returned to the well.

She was hanging over it, staring down into the blackness, and I was shocked at the malignancy in her face.

She wore the same expression I had seen so many times in Freidman's face. A triumphant leer of malicious hatred.

She hadn't heard me come back, and I caught her unawares. She spun around quickly, fearfully, the hatred slipping from her face to be replaced instantly by the passive, obedient expression I'd got to know so well.

I leaned over the lip of the well, levelled the torch and thumbed it to life. It was difficult to focus. Then, finally, deep, deep down, I saw the reflection of the torch on smooth black water that was evil, placid and secretive.

I straightened up, and I was trembling. Now that it was over, I was feeling the reaction, my knees rubbery.

She said, almost casually, like she did this every day: "Don't waste time. Let's get out of here."

We had to get as long a start as possible. We had a great advantage in that the shack was isolated. With luck, almost two weeks might pass before anyone suspected anything was wrong.

I thought about fingerprints, dropped the flat iron down the well to keep Freidman company. Then we spent half-an-hour boarding up the smashed window frame in the kitchen door. I scrawled on it in big chalk letters:

AWAY DUE TO ILLNESS. WILL ADVISE WHEN RETURN

That was for the benefit of the milkman, the baker, and any other tradesmen who might call.

It was almost dark by this time, but there was just one more thing I wanted to do. I opened the door of Freidman's bedroom, almost with a feeling of awe, wondering what I should see and why it was always locked so carefully.

I stared in amazement.

There couldn't possibly have been less furniture. Just the big, double bed, a chair and a clothes closet.

I opened the closet, pulled out the drawers, tumbled the contents on the floor. There was nothing except a few pieces of underclothing, spare sheets and a pile of old newspapers.

She was standing in the doorway, staring at me expressionlessly. She asked, in a dead voice: "What are you looking for?"

"Money," I grated. "We've got to have money. I figured he had a mountain of dough stacked away here."

"He took it into town every week," she said, dully. "Took it to the bank."

I pushed past her, out into the dining room, rang open the drawer of the cash till, counted the dough inside. It wasn't far short of fifty bucks.

I sighed, tucked the dough away in my pocket. "It's enough to last us a coupla days."

She said, emotionlessly: "Is there anything else you want? Or can we go?"

I gave a final look around. I hoped I'd thought of everything and was leaving the joint looking as though it had been closed temporarily.

"Anything *you* wanna bring?" I asked. "Anything you need?"

She looked down at her bare feet, no longer bleeding but caked with dried blood and dirt. "Nothing," she said, dully. "Nothing at all."

We found the car a mile down the road, where he had parked it before returning to catch us out.

I backed the car on to the road, checked the petrol supply, went around to the boot and unlocked that.

I sighed with relief. His attache case was in back there, and contained just over a thousand dollars. The money made me feel better, made everything so very much easier.

We bypassed Claremont, where Freidman had been banking, kept on driving. It was dark by now and the roads were deserted, long stretches for miles and miles without sight of a farm or a house. As it got late, we discovered our first mistake. We should have made sandwiches, brought them along with us. But we'd forgotten all about food until we were hungry and thirsty. And it was foolish to enter the few isolated eating houses we encountered. We didn't want anyone to remember us while we were in the vicinity of Freidman.

After I'd been driving for almost five hours, I pulled off the road into the scrub, turned off the engine and the lights.

"What happens now?" she asked, dully, wearily. She was like an automaton, talking and moving like a robot, emotionless and devoid of personality.

"Better catch up on some sleep," I warned her. "Even if you don't feel like sleeping, you've got to catch up on it. We've got some real hard travelling ahead of us."

I climbed in the back of the car, adjusted the car cushions to make ourselves comfortable. And after all this time, I was still dreaming, telling myself it wasn't true I'd killed Freidman, and that this nightmare flight through the darkness was merely an extension of my dream.

Then she was beside me, her head on my shoulder, her hot body pressing against mine. With a kinda physical shock, I realised what she wanted, what musta been dominating her mind ever since we'd left that place back there.

I almost recoiled from her.

She didn't notice my reaction. Her hot hands came for me from out of the darkness, insistent and searching, inspired and urgent, so that even while my mind revolted, my body was responding, softening and melting beneath the burning pressure of her lips, responding to the magic rhythm of her fingers.

It was like swimming effortlessly in a hot sea of pleasure, floating luxuriously while quivers of ecstasy rocked me gently and sensuously, feeling myself lifted higher and higher and higher towards the pinnacles of achievement, soaring upwards with a soft surge that was rapidly becoming faster and faster.

Then it was like a knifecord ripping into my brain. The sudden, sickening image of Freidman, his body doubled, his eyes glazed and his jaw sagging open.

It froze me, turned my blood ice-cold, paralysed me so that, for seconds, I was rigid. Then I was fighting her, clawing myself away, tearing myself from an embrace that suddenly had the cold, relentless and slimy touch of an octopus.

I fought myself out of the car door, stood leaning against it, panting and trembling. Through the darkness, I could sense her staring at me in a kinda scared wonder.

It wasn't a dream any more.

Freidman was dead. Was really dead!

And I had killed him!

I'd smashed in his skull, dropped his body in a deep well, and was now making a get-away.

I had Freidman's car, I had his money and I had his wife. And none of it was a dream. It was reality. Harsh reality.

She said, in a harsh, frightened whisper: "What's the matter with you? What's happened?"

My knees were weak, unable to take my weight. I sank to a sitting position, my shoulders resting against the car. I rested my head in my hands and started to cry like a child!

* * *

Early the next morning, we passed through a small town. A coupla miles further on, I ran the car off the road, on to the grass verge, walked back to town.

I kinda slunk in through the main street, full of guilt, sure everyone was watching us suspiciously, half guessing I was a killer, and had black fear living with me.

I shopped carefully and cautiously, not spending too much at one store. I bought myself a flannel shirt and slacks and a sports jacket. I put them on in the shop, had my old clothes tied up in a brown paper parcel. The first chance I got, I dumped my old clothes in a waste-bin.

Then I bought clothes for her, things she'd asked me to buy. A frock, brassiere, panties and shoes. Just enough to enable her to come into town herself and buy the things she needed.

I bought a rucksack, groceries and cans of beer, swung the load on to my shoulders and hiked out of town back to where I'd left her.

She was sitting in the car, looked as though she hadn't moved. Her complete lack of emotion was beginning to get me. She was cow-like, passive and accepting. Completely without life or imagination of her own.

I unpacked the food and we picnicked, eating wolfishly, glancing up guiltily every time a car passed. When we were through eating, I said anxiously: "We'd better get going. We don't want to attract attention hanging around too long."

I unpacked the frock I'd bought for her, went with her behind the hedge so she could change.

The sun was well overhead now, and it was strong. When she stripped off that old black frock, I could see clearly her strong tendency towards plumpness. Her breasts were over-heavy, kinda sagged as she thrust them into the brassiere, kinda overflowed her neckline. Her thighs were much thicker and sturdier than I'd realised, and the dress I'd bought for her was too small. It was a struggle for her to get into it, and it clung so tight that it seemed to emphasise the thickness of her thighs.

I was seeing her with new eyes, seeing her in a way I'd never seen her before. I was remembering the heat of that kitchen, the way the sweat had rolled out of her all day. And despite that, she was still plump. When she bent her head, buttoning her frock, I noticed the fine down on her upper lip, which in time would become a moustache. She was older than I'd first thought. Out in the open, I could see her age, the crows' feet at the corners of her eyes, the tiny wrinkles in her neck.

And, quite suddenly, she was ugly, repellent and loathsome. It was like I was in the company of a total stranger, someone whom I had never met before and who would always remain a stranger.

Yet we were bound together, united by a bond of guilt that couldn't be severed.

She pulled the dress down over her head, adjusted out the skirt. It was short, came to just above her plump knees. She asked, coyly: "How do I look?"

"You look good," I croaked. "Real good." I knew I had to string along, act towards her the way she expected.

She reached out with a hot hand, took mine. She deliberately hadn't buttoned the front of her dress yet. She purred softly. "You were upset last night, weren't you?"

"Yeah," I grunted, and I began to pant, because she had a way with her, a kinda animal instinct that was insistent, compelling and dominating.

She was hot and possessive, lips greedy, her hands throbbing.

"No," I panted desperately. "Not here. It's too close to the road."

She was clinging, using her weight to pull me down. Her lips were hot and wet, her body already felt moist with perspiration through the thin dress.

She was as strong as an animal, and her desire was unquenchable. Out in the open on the grass, in the midst of natural surroundings and away from the fear of Freidman, she lost herself completely.

She was consuming, devouring like some giant slug, draining the strength and life from me and sobbing for even more. Long after I lay still, she was moving restlessly, sighing with exasperation, her body jerking, hot, moist and burning.

As she lay beside me, I watched her from the corner of my eye. There were beads of perspiration dewing her forehead and the fine moustache on her upper lip. She lay on her side with her eyes closed, and I could see the curve of her cheek, a cheek that was too plump, breasts heavy and flabby, sagging lifelessly.

Worst of all, I could smell her. The hot smell of her perspiration soaking through her frock and the smell of her bad breath, acid and sickening.

112

I sat up abruptly, disgusted with myself, watched her and tried to conceal the loathing in my eyes.

She straightened out her skirt, climbed to her feet. She tried to smile coyly, rubbed up close against me, and I knew now that she was that type, always hungry, never satisfied.

"Put your shoes on," I grunted. "We've got to get going."

Immediately, she was passive and obedient, like being spoken to harshly was the only language she understood. She brushed the grass and twigs off the back of her frock, forced one plump, bare foot into one of the shoes. It was tight, made her wince with pain as she forced it on.

She didn't attempt to put on the other shoe. "The other," I growled. "You're supposed to wear two at the same time."

She showed me then the red, inflamed gash underneath the arch of her foot, clearly visible through the dried blood and dirt. I found a small stream, washed her foot clean. It looked a nasty wound, an inflamed surface with a darkly yellow tinted area deep down under the skin.

"You did this yesterday on the glass?"

She nodded dumbly. "It hurts," she said.

I took her feet between my hands, pressed my thumbs either side of the cut. She went rigid, moaned the way she moaned when Freidman tormented her. I kept on pressing. I was convinced there was a piece of glass embedded in her foot that was festering.

I couldn't get at it. It was deep down. I released her foot, wiped my forehead with the back of my hand.

"It's okay," she said, wincing. "It'll be better soon."

"That's what you think!"

"I've had cut feet before," she said, casually. "It'll go away."

She put on her shoe, limped back to the car. She sat beside me, held my arm as I coaxed the car back on the main drag and started heading further south.

"Where are we making for, honey?" she asked. Her head was on my shoulder, her hot fingers clasping my arm. From the corner of my eye, I could see her sprouting upper lip and flabby cheeks. The smell of her breath was nauseating and ...

"I've been thinking," I said.

113

"Yes, honey?" Her hands were hot and moist, moving ceaselessly. I was sick and disgusted with myself, found her touch loathsome and unpleasant.

"We've got to split up," I announced. "We'll have a better chance that way. Some time tonight, we'll ditch the car, split what dough we've got and each go our own way. Later, when things have cooled down, we can get together again."

There was a warning bell ringing so loudly in her head that I could almost hear it myself. The rigidity of her body, the sudden clenching of her fingers on my arm, expressed everything. She said in a low voice, astounding me with her foresight: "You want to get rid of me, don't you?"

"You're crazy," I protested. "What makes you think that?"

"You want to get rid of me, persuade me to go off by myself. That way, you think I'll get the blame. You want me to be accused of murder."

I strained out a weak laugh. "That's crazy talk. Where d'you get these ideas?"

She said slowly, like she was repeating a lesson she'd learned: "You've got to take care of me. You killed Freidman. Now you've got to take care of me, look after me, be with me all the time. That's what you promised. That's what you said you would do."

"Sure," I said. "That's what I'm gonna do. But it's better for the moment if we split up and ..."

Her fingers had an astonishing strength as they gouged into my arm. "You're not to leave me," she stated, flatly. "You're the only one I've got to look after me now. You're not going to leave me. You've got to be with me all the time. Understand?"

"Listen," I grated. "You can't tell me what I've got to do. You can't order me around."

She said quietly, emotionlessly: "The first instant you leave me, I shall go to the cops. I've got nothing to fear. I'll tell them the way you killed Freidman, the way you took his dough. I'll tell them everything."

A cold shiver ran down my spine. I tried to shake it off. "That's okay by me, honey, if that's the way you feel. But you're being crazy."

"Don't forget," she said, tonelessly, emotionlessly. "I've got nothing to lose. The moment you leave me, I go to the cops and tell them everything."

"Okay," I said, reluctantly. "You don't have to worry. I won't leave you. We'll stick together."

I could see my future unrolling before me. If we were lucky enough to avoid capture, we'd be settling down in some quiet town under a new name, me taking a job and working hard, while she was watching over me all the time, getting plumper and plumper, her neck fattening, her cheeks sagging down to her treble chin, the fine hairs on her upper lip turning into a thick moustache. And all the time, I'd be her companion, subjected to her greedy, merciless animal instincts, working by day to provide her with comfort, returning at nights to her greedy, insatiable, amorous and slug-like embraces.

And all the time, the fear would be hanging over me; just a few words from her and the cops would be investigating, digging, holding me on suspicion meanwhile.

"Don't worry, honey," I choked. "I won't leave you ever!" And for the first time in my life, I felt murder in my heart.

My mouth and lips were raw, like skin had been torn away in strips. My lungs were smouldering and I couldn't see through eyes that were painfully swollen.

The fat dick watched me spit the remains of the mustard from my mouth, held up a glass water jug, slowly poured water from it into a glass tumbler.

The sound was music in my ears, the desire for moisture for my dried-up body so strong that I wanted to scream, fall down on my knees and plead for just enough to moisten my lips.

He sipped from the glass, slowly and tantalisingly. All the time, he was watching me with black eyes full of hatred. The, he slowly up-ended the glass, and poured the precious water upon the stone floor. The sound and the sight of water being wasted almost drove me crazy.

"You were too generous with water, Farran," he snarled. "You gave Freidman a drink. A nice, long drink."

There was no rest, no conclusion to this torture. I wanted to die, to feel my pain-racked, agonised body turn stiff and cold, unresponsive to the merciless humiliations and tortures inflicted upon it.

"How d'you feel now, killer?" he grated.

I was going to faint. The knowledge of it crept over me like a shroud of peacefulness. I was going to slip down into that soft, white mist and sleep forever.

"You fancied Freidman's dame, didn't you?" ha snarled.

I didn't see him, but I sensed the gesture he made to the others, and as they moved in on me, I was smiling to myself, the white mist was gathering me up, gathering me into its embrace, cradling me, rocking me to sleep.

They couldn't hurt me now.

CHAPTER TWELVE

Three days later, we were twenty miles north of the Mexican border.

As far as I could discover, we were still unsuspected. I'd been buying all the newspapers and listening to all the newsflashes on the radio. There hadn't been the slightest mention of Freidman.

But the States is a mighty big continent. If the newspapers printed everything that occurred in every city, they'd have to print a daily edition as bulky as the Domesday Book.

We looked around for an estate agent, said we were taking a long holiday, and rented a small cabin way out of town near one of the lakes. It was the wrong time of the year for a holiday, and the estate agent was suspicious. But I paid him a month in advance, and that took care of all his worries.

But it didn't take care of my worries.

As soon as we were inside the cabin, she limped across to one of the bunks, stretched out on it and moaned. Her face was grey.

I eased off her shoe, gently and carefully. She wasn't gonna get that shoe on again, not the way her foot was swollen. She'd known that and had refused to take her shoe off this last coupla days. And now I could see her foot, I felt sick.

The whole of the underside of her foot was a kinda yellowy-green colour, like it was rotting away.

"You're crazy," I told her. "You've got to see a doctor."

She shook her head, obstinately. "We can't risk it," she panted. "Doctors ask questions, want security numbers, might even wanna send me to hospital. We can't risk it. We mustn't give anyone a clue to where we are."

I took one more look at her foot, got up and went over to the door.

She propped herself up on her elbows, almost screamed at me: "Where are you going?"

"To get a doctor."

She said quietly: "Come back here." But she said it in such a way that I was scared to disobey.

I sat beside her on the bunk for a few moments. She said softly: "Do what I tell you. Get a knife, a sharp knife."

I guessed what was in her mind and shuddered.

"What's the matter with you," she snarled. "You weren't scared when you killed Freidman. This won't take a minute. Get a knife, damn you!"

I went through to the kitchen, found a small, sharp kitchen knife. There was methylated spirits in the medicine cabinet. I poured a little into a saucer, set it on fire and held the blade of the knife in the flame.

When I got back to her, she was writhing in pain. I had to wait until the spasm had passed away. She groped for me with a hot hand, clutched my arm. "What are you waiting for," she croaked. "D'you want me to die?"

Die!

DIE!

If she died, it would solve all my problems. Then maybe I could cross the frontier into Mexico, set myself free for all time from fear of arrest. She was a weight around my neck, a weight that would weigh me down for the rest of my life, bind me hand and foot, chain me inescapably to my crimes for the rest of my life.

And it would be so simple. She was weak now, hadn't the strength to help herself. I could lock the door on her, drive away in the car, leave her until the poison took effect, climbed up her leg and entered into her blood-stream and caused the rest of her body to rot as her foot was now rotting.

"For God's sake," she pleaded.

I gritted my teeth, went to the foot of the bed, sat on the edge of it, took her foot between my hands and gripped it tight between my thighs.

It was worse than I had thought it would be. As the keen knife edge sliced cleanly across the inflamed, discoloured flesh, her foot seemed to explode. Blood and pus spurted on to the floor and on to my hands. I was sick, wanted to vomit, but knew I must keep a grip on myself, knew I must finish what had to be done.

I gouged my thumbs into the festering wound, gouged and pressed, squeezing out the matter. And she was arching in agony, biting her own arm like a wolf as she fought against the pain. I probed with the knife, kept probing, the sweat trickling down my forehead into my eyes. And I couldn't find anything, couldn't find the root of the poison.

Then the agony became so intense it was unbearable. Her hands gouged into my neck and shoulders, forcing me away from her.

I went outside and was a long time being very, very sick. When I felt better, I walked down to the lake, washed myself again and again to rid myself of the smell and touch of festering matter.

When I got back to the cabin, she was lying there with eyes wide open, breathing so softly that at first I was afraid she wasn't breathing at all.

She said in a tight, controlled voice: "Can you find some disinfectant?"

I'd bought a bottle of rye as well as groceries at the last town we'd passed. I had to steel myself to sit beside her again, and tried not to see the mess on the floor. I swabbed the wound with raw spirits while she gritted her teeth.

There was still pus in the wound. I couldn't clean it away. And I could see the slither of glass now, buried deep down in the foot. But I couldn't get at it, could only just touch it with the point of the knife. She couldn t stand the pain of me digging for it.

I bound up her foot with my handkerchief, brought a bucket and water from the kitchen and cleaned up the floor.

When I was through, she said quietly: "Most of the pain's gone now. It'll get better soon."

I said, insistently: "We've got to go into town, go see a doctor."

"We'll see," she said. "We'll see." She swung her legs around off the bunk, sat up, tried to give me a smile.

"That's not the only trouble," I told her. "We've got to start thinking hard. We're almost out of dough. Just the food we've got with us and a little over."

She stared at me incredulously. "A thousand bucks! All gone?"

"We've got enough for maybe the next two weeks," I said. "But we've almost hit bottom. With petrol, the clothes you needed, food and the rent of this cabin, the dough's just melted away.

She said, with a kinda frightened note in her voice: "But we've got to live. We've got to get some dough from somewhere."

"And another thing," I told her. "Freidman's car. It's hot. We've got to find some way to ditch it."

"Can't we sell it?" she asked, hopefully.

I shot her a contemptuous look. During the past three days, I'd not only found her repellent, I'd found her stupid, ignorant and mulishly obstinate. "There's such a thing as number plates," I grated. "The new owner's name has to be registered. We've got to ditch that car and quick. Maybe set it on fire. Get rid of it someway so it won't be traced."

"What are we going to do about money?" she said, worriedly, coming back to the main difficulty.

"I don't know," I said, hopelessly. "I just don't know."

She said, slowly and deliberately: "We've got to have money; you understand that, don't you? We've got to have money."

"Sure," I said, weakly. "I understand." I was thinking that travelling alone, I could make it, maybe get over into Mexico, manage with a few bucks until I could find myself a niche. Maybe I could leave her anyway. We were twenty miles from the border. A quick hop over and I'd be free of the cops, free of her too.

"We've got to get money!" she said, insistently.

"How?" I asked.

She said slowly, meaningfully: "Some guys get money when they want. There's always ways to get money."

I stared at her, eyes wide.

"Well, why not?" she rasped. "You robbed Freidman of his dough, didn't you? What you've done once, you can do again."

I went over to the table, picked up the bottle of rye, took a long gulp from it. The liquor stung my mouth, made my eyes smart. I brushed the back of my hand across my mouth, walked over to the door.

She shouted quickly: "Where are you going?"

"I'm going for a drive," I told her. "Get some fresh air. I wanna think."

She said, ominously: "Be back within an hour. I mean what I say. Be back within an hour. If you're not, I'll be on my way to the nearest call-box. They'll pick you up in no time."

"They'll have you too," I snarled.

She shook her head, smiled craftily. "Not the way I'll tell the story," she said.

I stood in the doorway, eyeing her. She stared back. It was me who gave first. I dropped my eyes, went out, didn't even close the door behind me.

I stumbled over to the car, climbed in behind the wheel. She'd given me an hour. It wasn't long enough to cross the frontier. Maybe she was even smart enough to figure that. I'd need to wait until night before I tried to cross the border illegally. Long before that, she'd have the cops on the alert for me.

I turned the ignition key, thumbed the engine into life and coaxed the car along the gravel drive, out on to the main drag. I just had to have time to think, time to find a way out of this mess.

The icy coldness against my forehead was hammering again and again at my brain, washing away the night to bring day, forcing consciousness to the surface.

It was ice they were holding to my head, pressing against my flesh until my temples became numbed, the numbness creeping into my brain, and night itself beginning to burn, burning hotter and hotter like a branding iron.

The fat dick said: "You ain't gonna escape so easy, Farran. There's a hundred ways we've got of bringing a guy round."

The coldness was a band of steel being relentlessly tightened, compressing my brain, squeezing and crushing until my mind was turned into a hard icicle. An icicle so cold it shrivelled my brain.

"We're not blind killers like you are, Farran," he gloated. "We're more subtle."

The steel band was biting into the core of the icicle, making it split and splinter, every fragment a searing white-hot agony.

"Why did you kill the dame, Farran," he snarled. " You killed Freidman to get her, didn't you? Why did you kill her?"

CHAPTER THIRTEEN

He didn't look up when I was shown into his surgery. He went on writing, said tiredly: "Will you be seated, please?"

I perched on the edge of a chair, saw the weariness in his lined forehead and his tired eyes.

He asked, wearily: "What seems to be the trouble?"

"You're needed, doctor," I said. "Somebody's ill."

"What name is it?" he asked, reaching for his index cards.

"A new patient," I told him.

"What are the symptoms?" he asked, taking up his pen to write.

"Looks like a badly poisoned foot."

He put down his pen, clasped his hands together in front of him and looked up at me for the first time. His eyes were a kinda bluey-grey, stared through me expressionlessly. "Sounds like a case for the hospital."

"I do wish you'd see her, doctor," I pleaded. "I feel sure she'd be much happier."

"I'm very busy," he said.

"It would make all the difference if you would come and see her," I urged.

"Where is she?" he sighed, reaching for his pen again.

"Out on Lakeside."

His hand stopped reaching, dropped back on the desk. "Did you say Lakeside?"

"Yeah." I was sweating.

"That's twelve miles."

"I've got my car outside," I said eagerly. "We can be there in no time."

I could see he wasn't gonna do it. He said: "If you've got a car, you'd better bring her into town."

"She's bad," I said. "Can't walk."

"She can hobble to a car."

"It's ... she's kinda ... semi-conscious."

His blue-grey eyes seemed to penetrate my brain.

"If she's that bad, son, you'll have to get her to hospital right away."

I went on trying. "If you would only come out and see her, bring your bag along, I'm sure you could fix her up good. Then she'd be out there in the open air, where it's healthy. Hospitals are kinda depressing."

His voice became sharp, just a little authoritative. "Now listen to me, son. A poisoned foot isn't to be played around with. You get her into hospital as quick as you know how. The infection will need to be cleaned out, dressings will have to be changed regularly."

There was a knock, and the white-uniformed receptionist poked her head around the door, beckoned to him.

"Excuse me a minute," he said.

He crossed the room, spoke to her in undertones for a few moments. Then he went out, closed the door behind him.

He wasn't going to do anything to help. And his talk about a hospital was scaring me. It was so easy for him, to bring along a local anaesthetic with him and probe for that piece of glass. When that was rooted out, she'd be okay.

I found I was staring at a pad on his desk, a printed pad of prescription forms with his signature already written on them.

Then suddenly I saw the solution; if I could give her something to kill the pain, so she could keep still while I probed for that shaft of glass, I'd be able to cut it out myself.

It was so easy and so natural, I didn't even know I was doing it, until I was sitting back in my chair with two or three blank signed prescription certificates in my pocket.

When he came back, he was preoccupied, glanced at me as though he'd forgotten who I was, what I wanted.

"Won't you come, doctor?" I pleaded.

He remembered then. He reached for his telephone. "I'll fix you up with a hospital right away, son. Tell me where you are and I'll have an ambulance call."

I got up quickly, nervously. "I guess I don't want to give all that trouble, doctor. I'll bring her in the car. We'll make it, all right."

"That's the idea, son," he said, with relief. "No sense in taking risks when there are hospitals."

I got out of there quick, the blank prescription forms burning a hole in my pocket. I knew it was no good just writing what I wanted. Doctors have their own methods of writing. I had to do this right, just the way a doctor would do it. In any case, I didn't know what was the best drug to kill pain.

I found the public library, went to the reference room and got down the books on drugs.

It appeared that morphia was the most efficient of the drugs, killing pain without unpleasantness for the patient. Laboriously and with great care, I copied the formula on to the prescription form.

I submitted it to a chemist at the other end of town, and my fingers were trembling when I handed over the prescription form.

The assistant gave the prescription form a casual glance, disappeared into the back of the shop, came out a few seconds later with his forehead puckered.

He asked, in a doubtful voice: "Did Dr Williams write this prescription himself?"

I went hot first, then icy-cold. I clenched my hands, felt them sweating. I said, hoarsely: "He was busy at the time. His assistant made it out."

To my relief, he nodded with satisfaction. "I thought it wasn't his handwriting," he said, pleased with his perspicacity. He gave me the tablets; round, mottled tablets the size of a dime and a dozen in a tube.

She hadn't been kidding about giving me an hour. I met her a coupla miles away from the cabin, hobbling painfully along the road, her face set and hard.

I drew up alongside her. "What the hell are you doing?" I demanded.

"I warned you," she said menacingly. "And you're lucky. If a car had picked me up, I'd have gone straight to police headquarters."

I got out, helped her into the car. She was having a lot of pain with that foot. I said bitterly: "You don't trust me, do you?"

"I can't afford to."

I got the car rolling. "I've been to a doctor," I told her. "I told him you were in pain. He's given me tablets to kill the pain."

"He's not coming here, is he?" she demanded anxiously.

"He wouldn't come all this way, even if I paid him," I said bitterly. "If he'd have come, I'd have brought him."

She changed the subject abruptly. "Have you thought about dough. We're gonna need dough."

I hadn't time to think. "I've been looking over a place," I told her, on the spur of the moment. "It should be a knockover. A garage. We can do it together, late one night when your foot's better."

"It'd better be soon," she grumbled.

When we got back to the cabin, I had to half-carry her inside. She lay on the bunk exhausted, and I could tell she'd used nearly all her strength hobbling that coupla miles along the road.

I dug down in my pocket, drew out the packet the chemist had wrapped up for me.

"Take these," I said. "They're supposed to kill the pain. Later maybe I can dig down for that piece of glass."

She looked at me suspiciously. "You're not trying to poison me, are you?"

I grinned at her. "D'you think I could ask a chemist for something to poison you? D'you think he'd just hand it over? Grow up, can't you? These tablets are only sold against a doctor's prescription."

She tore open the wrapping, examined the tablets suspiciously. "What do I have to do?"

"Take one when the pain is bad."

"The pain's bad now."

"Then take one," I told her. "They're supposed to kill pain. Then, when the pain has eased, I'll start digging."

She took a tablet, washed it down with water. She corked the tube, put it on the table at the side of the bunk.

"Feeling hungry ?" I asked.

She nodded.

"I'll throw a few eggs together to make an omelette," I told her.

I didn't know much about drugs, so I kept watching her to see what reaction the tablet had. It didn't seem to have much effect, except that after eating she yawned, said she felt sleepy.

"How's the pain?"

"Not so bad. Foot's kinda numbed."

"How about another tablet?"

She reached for the tube, shook another tablet into her hand. Not long afterwards, she went to sleep, breathing kinda heavily and moving restlessly.

I cleared away the dirty crockery, went through to the kitchen and washed up.

When I came back, she was snoring.

I sat on the edge of the bed, stripped off the wrapping around her foot and felt sick again when I saw the raw, festering edges of the wound.

I touched it with my finger and she moaned a little, stirred, opened her eyes, and said irritably, but sleepily: "Don't do that. It hurts."

"I've got to do it," I said.

"You mustn't," she half-wailed. She was crying.

I went back to the kitchen, sterilised the sharp, pointed kitchen knife in methylated spirits and went back to her.

"You've got to try and take it," I warned her.

"It hurts," she moaned.

I started probing, and I could feel her body vibrating, kinda quivering as she turned her head from side to side. But now she hadn't the strength to push me away.

I got it at last, pried it loose, a slender shaft of glass, sticky with blood and pus. As it came loose, the blood gushed freely and she screamed, clawed my back with flailing finger nails.

I swabbed again with disinfectant, tried to swab away the yellowing, festering edges. But she was rolling about in pain now, writhing so much that I couldn't hold her still. I gave up, found fresh handkerchiefs, bound up her foot.

She went to sleep soon after that, waking up at intervals to ask me the time and staring at me with a strange, dazed expression in her eyes.

"How's the foot," I asked, the next time she woke up.

"It's numb," she said. "But painful."

"It'll be better soon," I told her reassuringly. "It's getting better now."

She sighed, closed her eyes, went to sleep again.

I read the evening papers, and a little later prepared the evening meal. She didn't want to eat, kept moaning with the pain of her foot. Finally, she said: "Those tablets did me good. I'd better have another."

I got her a glass of water and she took another tablet. It seemed to give her a psychological uplift. As soon as she'd taken it, she lay back in the bunk, closed her eyes, and her face was kinda soothed.

It musta been in the early hours of the morning when she started whimpering.

It woke me.

I could hear her through the darkness across the room. I called out to her. "What is it? What's happening?"

"The pain," she whispered hoarsely. "The pain!"

"Take a tablet," I said.

I could hear her fumbling for the tube, heard it click on the table as she replaced it. After that, she settled comfortably, went off to sleep.

But the tablets weren't strong enough. Dawn was breaking when her whimpering aroused me again. I climbed out of bed sleepily, crossed over to her. She was twisting her head from side to side, clenching her hands tightly together, her face contorted in a grimace of agony.

I unwound the bandage from her foot, felt sick when I saw it. The greeny-yellowy area had expanded. Yellowy shoots were climbing her leg towards her knee.

I said hoarsely: "Listen to me. You've got to go to hospital. Understand? I'm gonna take you to hospital."

"No," she persisted. "I'll be all right. I just need something to kill the pain. I'll take another tablet."

She took another tablet. That left just six in the tube. But this time, the tablet didn't seem to have any effect. She lay there whimpering with pain, whimpering so I couldn't stand it any longer.

"I'm going out to have a swim," I told her. "When I get back, if you're no better, I'm taking you to hospital.

Understand? Whatever happens, I'm taking you to hospital."

"No. Not the hospital," she pleaded.

I went for a long walk through the woods and down to the lake, following it for miles, figuring the way I was gonna work it. I'd take her to hospital, book her in under an assumed name, promise her I'd see her at visiting time the next day. Then I'd slip off quietly.

I didn't know what conditions were in Mexico, but I figured I'd be able to find myself a job.

The snag was that she was smart enough to realise I wanted to get free from her. Unless I was smooth enough and convincing, she might get too smart, start talking to the hospital officials as soon as I'd left, and set the cops on me.

Yeah, she was smart. She knew already her disadvantage in being in hospital. That was why she was so determined not to go.

All the time I'd been walking, I hadn't seen a soul. I stripped off my clothes, waded into the lake, found it cold but refreshing. I swam around for maybe half-an-hour, climbed back into my clothes and set off back to the cabin.

It was almost dusk when I arrived there, and I was ravenously hungry.

There were no lights burning. I went in, closed the door behind me, and just for a moment, my heart gave a jump of fear as I thought she wasn't there. Then I heard her soft breathing, saw the dim bulk of her huddled on the bunk.

I switched on the lights, said loudly: "Are you awake?"

She didn't say anything.

I crossed over to her, stared down at her. Her eyes were kinda half-open, showing the whites. She turned her head ceaselessly on the pillow.

I shook her shoulder. "Hey," I said. "How about some eats. Hungry?"

She stared up at me with a kinda remote expression in her eyes, almost as though I was a stranger. Then she started turning her head from side to side again.

"Listen?" I demanded. "Are you all right?"

She closed her eyes, took a deep breath, sighed, began to sink down into a deep sleep.

I looked at the bedside table. The tube containing the tablets was empty. It wasn't difficult to realise what had happened. She'd been having a lot of pain, and the effects of the first few tablets had worn off quickly. Now she needed a stronger dose to kill the pain.

I mentally shrugged my shoulders. Maybe it was a good thing she'd used them all. If I let her sleep off the effects of the tablets, she'd have to go to hospital. The pain of her foot alone would make her insist on it.

She lay like a log while I stripped off the bandage and examined her foot. It wasn't getting any better. I washed it again with whisky, re-bandaged it, went through to the kitchen and carefully washed my hands After that, I prepared myself a meal.

She was sleeping quietly now, peacefully. I turned off the light, climbed into bed and lay awake a long time, listening to her breathing softly. I was making plans for my future!

The next thing I knew was the sunlight streaming in through the window.

I blinked a coupla times, stretched my arms and started fighting the temptation to remain between the sheets. There was a persistent nag at the back of my mind. Something not quite right. I couldn't place what it was, and it worried me.

I got up, padded through to the kitchen, washed under the tap and towelled myself briskly. Then I switched on the electric toaster, started brewing coffee.

While the water was getting hot, I went back to wake her up.

It was when I was near enough to touch her that I realised with a shock what was nagging at the back of my mind.

I couldn't hear the sound of her breathing!

There was an icy hand around my heart. For seconds, I stood paralysed, before I summoned up the courage to reach out, touch her shoulder.

Her shoulder was kinda hard, cold. I recoiled from her and backed a coupla paces, stared at her unbelievingly.

The clock on the mantelpiece ticked solemnly. It was the only thing that moved. Everything else was silent, waiting, brooding, almost as though watching my reactions.

I hadn't the courage to touch her again. I circled around so I could see her face. Her eyes were open, glazed, just the way Freidman's eyes had been open. The tip of her tongue protruded through her teeth, and it was bloodless, white, like a piece of flannel.

I couldn't believe it!

I stumbled through to the kitchen, found a bottle of Scotch, drank half a tumblerful to try and stop my hands from shaking.

I wasn't fooling myself. I hadn't any affection for that dame. I didn't want to see her die. I didn't want to see anyone die. But she had died, and there was nothing I could do about it.

I was beginning to realise the angles, was realising the medical book hadn't been exaggerating when it said an overdose of morphia could result in death.

And there were guys who were going to start asking questions. For example, how did she obtain those tablets? Who had given them to her? Why had he given them to her?

The answers added up in a way I didn't like. They added up in a way that put me in a sweat, made me realise with startling clearness that I didn't ought to waste any time. I had to get out of the States as quickly as possible, cross the boundary into Mexico, even if I had to do so with bullets whistling around my ears.

I forgot about breakfast. I dressed hurriedly, counted my dough, gathered my belongings together and packed everything in an attache case.

I purposely didn't look at her as I closed the door of the cabin behind me. I didn't want to be put into that cold sweat again. Almost unseeingly, unsteadily, I walked over to Freidman's car, climbed inside and switched on the ignition.

It was a short, bumpy ride down the winding gravel drive to the main drag. When I neared the end of the drive, I saw another car swinging in off the main drag. There wasn't room for the two of us to pass.

I stopped and waited.

The other car braked, straddled across the road in front of me. There were two guys in the car, both wearing grey fedoras. They climbed out, circled around on either side of me.

I couldn't go on, because they were blocking the road, and it was useless reversing back to the cabin.

One of them rested his foot on the running board, leaned his arms on my open window. He said, conversationally: "This your car, son?"

I was trembling inside. I was thinking of her, back there in the cabin. I wasn't gonna be happy until I'd got plenty of distance between her and me.

"Yeah," I said. "What's it got to do with you?"

While we were talking, the other guy had opened the other door, was checking the licence tag. It had Freidman's name on it.

"Hey," I growled. "What the hell d'you think you're doing?"

The guy nearest me put his hand in his hip pocket, produced a wallet, flicked it open long enough for me to see the badge inside.

I started to sweat.

He said: "Just climb out the car a moment, will you, son? We've got a coupla questions we wanna ask."

There was nothing I could do. There was one of them either side of me.

I shrugged my shoulders, climbed down from behind the steering wheel.

The guy who'd done all the talking asked: "So this is your car?"

"Sure," I said, doggedly. "Why. What's the trouble?"

"What's your name, son?"

"Morris," I said quickly. "Ted Morris."

He said, casually: "You wouldn't know a guy named Freidman, would you?"

There was a kinda numbed hopelessness inside me. I knew that it was useless lying. If I said I didn't know Freidman, their next question would be why I was in possession of Freidman's car.

I said quickly: "That's the guy you want to ask," and nodded over their shoulders. As they automatically turned their heads, I made a break for it.

They were too wise to be caught by an old trick like that. A foot hooked itself between my ankles, brought me down hard, the palms of my hands smacking the ground and all the breath pounded out of my chest.

They stood over me.

"Your name's Farran, ain't it, son?" growled one, and an ugly note had crept into his voice.

I didn't know cops could be so smart. I didn't know they could track a guy down so easily, find out his name, even know what he was thinking. And the grim realisation that these were cops and I was their prisoner, drove me frantic. I had to get away, I had to escape.

Just twenty miles to Mexico and I'd be free!

I bunched my feet together, lashed out, kicked the ankles away from under one of them. Then I was on my feet, running like a hunted stag, heading back towards the cabin where she was lying.

The dick chasing me musta won prizes for running. Fear was winging my feet, allowing me but one blind thought – escape!

But just the same, the other dick outran me, clamped a heavy hand on my shoulder, wrenched me around, twisted me so I spun off balance, fell to the ground.

The next moment he was straddled across me, the weight of his knees pinioning my upper arms, the weight of his body grinding into my chest.

I looked up into his hard, grim face, saw the hatred in his eyes. "So you're Farran," he snarled. "You're the killer. You're the guy who knocked off Freidman."

"You don't understand," I quavered. "You don't understand ..."

"Aw, shuddup," he growled, and the palm of his hand smacked my face from side to side, hard. I vaguely sensed it was all he could do to restrain himself from using his knuckles.

The other dick came panting up. He was limping. "So you've got the little bastard," he snarled.

"I'll say I've got him!"

There was the clink of chain, the glint of bright metal in the sun, and then my hands were being clamped together, steel bracelets pinioning my wrists.

"All right, get him on his feet so we can have a good look at him." It was the dick whose ankles I'd kicked. He looked good and sore.

They dragged me to my feet. I stood there, half-fainting with fear and desperation.

"Look at him, a killer. A ruthless killer. Look at him now. Yella. Yella through and through."

"But you don't understand ..." I began, half sobbing.

"Here's something you can understand."

A fist exploded in my solar plexus. Then, as my body jack-knifed, a knee came up, smashed against my nostrils.

I went down in a red blur, hearing blood and bone spurting and grinding, sensing through a mist of pain their hands grasping my arms, dragging me to my feet.

"Stop crying," sneered an ugly voice. "There's a reception committee down at headquarters. Once you get there, you'll have a real reason to cry."

CHAPTER FOURTEEN

"Why did you poison the dame, Farran?"

I was sinking in a sea of pain, tethered to the chair by my wrists and ankles. A fist slammed against my jaw when I didn't answer, but the sound was remote, and I felt almost nothing.

"What made you kill the dame, Farran?"

When I didn't reply, his fist impacted again.

I wanted them to kill me. I wanted to die so I wouldn't have to continue living in this agonised hell.

Then, through the mist of pain, I sensed the sudden change of atmosphere. A door opening, the cop captain, his voice worried and insistent.

"They've finally got through," he said. "I can't block them any longer. There's an attorney outside with a sanction signed by the Senator. He wants to see him right away."

The voices were indistinct, far, far away. I heard the fat dick sigh. "We haven't got going yet."

The cop captain rasped: "You've got to get him cleaned up, make him presentable. He must see his attorney. And his attorney is Greig Scotland."

The fat dick drew in a deep breath of dismay. "Greig Scotland!"

"Yeah," grunted the cop captain. "You've got less than half-an-hour to get him cleaned up. I can't stall Greig any longer than that. You'd better have a good story ready, too."

I was as weak as a kitten. They unpinioned my wrists and ankles, stripped off my clothes, sluiced me down with ice-cold water. Somebody found me a clean shirt, and they dragged me back to my cell, tidied me, somebody even combing my hair.

The fat dick stood over me, scowling menacingly.

"You've just had a taste of what we can do, Farran", he said.

I looked at him through battered, half-closed eyes. I didn't say anything. I was too weak and too beaten, every spark of life crushed outta me.

"It's a pity we had to beat you up this way," he said, with a mirthless grin. "But you shouldn't have tried to escape."

I didn't say anything, just hung my head and prayed silently that they would leave me alone.

The cop captain stuck his head in the cell door. "Are you through?" he demanded, anxiously. "I can't stall him any longer. He's getting ready to phone the Senator."

"Okay, bring him in," growled the fat dick.

Greig Scotland was one of the tallest guys I've ever seen, lanky and soulful-looking. He had thick, black hair smarmed down hard on his head, and the cheerfulness of an undertaker. His eyes were set wide apart, were black and fathomless.

He stood in the doorway of the cell, looked first at me with the merest flicker of interest and then switched his eyes to the fat dick.

"So it's you, Maclean," he rasped, bitterly.

The fat dick snarled. "So what if it is?"

Greig Scotland said: "Up to the same tricks?"

Maclean grinned slowly, viciously. "You know the kid's reputation," he said. "He's a killer. We had to rough him up a bit to persuade him along to headquarters."

Greig Scotland looked at me, looked at Maclean. Then he crossed over to me with long, lanky strides, looked down into my face. "You're making an art of it, Maclean," he said, softly. "A pile-driver couldn't have done better."

Maclean grinned mockingly. "Maybe you'd like to take a hand yourself."

Greig looked at him solemnly. He said in a quiet, even voice: "I'm going to get you for this, Maclean. This time, it's only a kid. You've been holding him for three days, blocking every application I've made to interview him. But this time, you've over-reached yourself. You've picked on a kid, and I'm gonna break you for it. Because this kid is gonna stand trial, and I'm gonna make him tell exactly what happened in that sweat room. I mean it, Maclean. This time I'm gonna break you."

There was a glint of uneasiness in Maclean's eyes, but he grinned impudently. "Try and make it stick," he invited. "Try and get sympathy for the kid. He's a killer. Everyone knows he's a killer. Everyone knows what he's been getting here, he richly deserves. Try and break me if you can."

Greig looked at me, looked at Maclean and then looked at the door. "Outside," he said, tersely. "I wanna see my client alone. Outside, all of you."

"And one other thing," said Maclean. "Just a friendly tip. Before you start shouting about the kid, remember this might break *you*. No one is gonna like seeing a kid killer defended."

"Outside," gritted Greig Scotland. "Outside, all of you."

When the door had closed behind them, he walked over to the tiny, barred window. He was tall enough to see out through it. He kept his shoulders turned to me, stood in silence for some minutes.

I sat there on the bunk and waited numbly. I wanted to die, and die quickly. I just hoped this guy wouldn't keep me too long.

He said, in a voice that was surprisingly soft: "I've seen your mother and father. They want me to act for you."

There was numb bitterness inside me. Home and all that it meant seemed so very far away.

"You don't want to talk about them?" he said, shrewdly.

"No," I choked, and there were tears pricking at the back of my eyes.

There was silence for another few minutes. "I'm here to defend you, Farran. To see you get justice. But there's questions I've got to ask you. Will you answer them?"

"Yeah," I said, bleakly.

"Did you run down those two girls after you'd been drinking and then drive on without stopping?"

"No," I said. "You see ..."

"We'll come to explanations later. For the moment, just answer my questions."

"Yes," I said, numbly.

"And did you run away instead of going to the police to report the accident?"

"Yeah," I said.

His voice was serious. "Had you been drinking much?"

"Not much," I said. "I wasn't drunk, if that's what you want to know."

"Your friends say you were drinking from a whisky bottle, you were driving with one hand, holding the whisky bottle in the other hand at the time of the accident."

"It's not true," I said dully, but without hope. I could see just the way they'd built it up when I ran away, protected themselves.

"Did you kill Freidman?"

"Yeah," I said, hopelessly. "You see ..."

"Explanations later. Just facts now. You admit you killed Freidman?"

"Yeah," I said, hollowly.

"And his wife. You were making love to her, he caught you making love to her, and it was then that you killed Freidman?"

I was reliving in my imagination that scene, her shocking screams and his awful, terrifying purpose. "Yeah," I croaked. "It was because of her I killed him."

"And you killed her, too?"

"No," I whimpered. "I didn't kill her."

"But you forged a prescription, obtained morphia tablets illegally, the same tablets that caused her death?"

"Yeah," I admitted.

"But you didn't kill her?"

"No," I said.

He sighed, drew a cigarette case from his pocket, turned around and offered me a cigarette. When I refused, he lit his own.

"We've got all the time in the world, Farran," he said quietly. "I want your full story now. I want your side of what happened. Don't leave out anything. I don't intend to protect you in any way from the justice of the law. But I'm going to see you obtain the full protection the law offers you. So start talking. Tell me everything. And don't leave out a thing."

I swallowed, nodded towards the cell door. "About what they did to me, too?"

"Everything," he said quietly. "Everything."

CHAPTER FIFTEEN

From where I sat in the dock, I could see my parents if I turned my head. I didn't turn my head. I couldn't bear to see them.

Immediately opposite me sat the jury, and I was watching them furtively, as though by looking at them directly, the judge would know I was pleading with them to help me.

My future was all in the hands of the jury, because it was a capital charge. The charge of homicide. The case had been running for three days, and I'd been listening to the prosecution building up a strong case against me, witness after witness stepping into the box and giving evidence.

It shocked me to hear that evidence, to learn how little actions and thoughtless phrases can be misconstrued.

Harry and Johnny were there, too. They hadn't once looked at me while giving evidence. They'd worked out their story between them, and stuck to it grimly. But Greig Scotland hammered at them again and again, cross-examined them until they stammered, contradicted themselves, and adjusted it to somewhere near the truth.

The trucker was the witness who shocked me most, because he had been a peeping tom, watched us through the crack in the door, exaggerated what happened.

Then came the evidence of the doctor. He said I'd been reluctant to send her to hospital, said I'd sat in his surgery arguing until he had to leave the room on business. In his absence, I'd taken the opportunity to steal the prescription forms.

Yeah, sitting in the dock and listening to all the evidence and trying to put myself in the place of the jury made me feel lower and lower.

Because things were different now. I no longer wanted to die. I wanted to live. Because, although I was in prison, I wasn't being tortured. Life was bearable, and I was young.

Then, finally, Greig Scotland climbed to his feet to begin his summing up. I knew now I should not remain long in doubt.

For two hours, the public sat spellbound listening to Greig Scotland. I listened with numbed anxiety.

Greig Scotland's low, melodic voice droned on and on, reciting in simple words the true facts as I'd given them to him, the plain, unvarnished truth, telling of my fears, my hates, my cowardice, my inner emotions, and of the beating I'd received in police headquarters.

Now he was coming to an end, describing how he'd come to police headquarters with a signed permit to interview me, how he had obtained an interview in my cell, sat opposite me while, bruised and battered and dazed with pain, I'd given him my account of what happened, just the way he was giving it to the court at that very moment.

I riveted my eyes on Scotland's shoulders. He was my hope, my one and only hope. And, as he reached the end of his summing-up, he paused, glanced down for a moment at the sheaf of notes he carried in his hand, and then looked directly at the jury.

He said in a clear, ringing voice: "There has been much newspaper talk about Farran being a mad killer, a mad dog, a man – no, a boy who justly merits execution! I say to you, men of the world as you are, that we are not always what we want to be. Circumstances help to make the man, and make him better or worse. By the force of circumstances, Farran finds himself standing in the dock today, his future in your hands."

He paused again, looked at me for a moment, went on. "I have told you Farran's story the way he told it to me. And ladies and gentlemen of the jury, I submit that any of you might have found yourselves in his position. He is young and inexperienced, and by force of circumstances, found himself driven inevitably along a path that even a strong-minded adult would have found it difficult to traverse."

Greig Scotland sat down so quietly that no-one in the court at first realised he had concluded his summing-up.

Then came the clearing of throats, a general movement among the public as they relaxed, the rustle of papers and whispers between counsels.

I could sense my mother and father looking at me hopefully, willing me to look at them. But I couldn't face them. I kept my head averted, deliberately lowered my eyes.

Then the judge's gavel was hammering on the table, the whispers and rustlings died away, the judge cleared his throat, looked at the jury, gave them a short but simple address.

I'd been through it all now. It was all over. All over except for the reckoning. I'd been stupid and I'd been foolish. But, as Greig Scotland had said, circumstances had been against me.

Everything that happened to me now was in the lap of the gods. Whatever was to be my destiny was in the hands of others.

The jury were rising to their feet and filing out solemnly. I watched them with my heart fluttering. They were ordinary folk, tradesmen and housewives. And as they left the court, I was addressing an unspoken prayer to them.

I didn't mind much what happened to me now. I'd suffered so much that punishment couldn't harm me more. But I did want those people to understand one thing.

I wanted them to know I wasn't a killer.

I wanted the whole world to know I wasn't a killer. I wanted everyone to understand exactly how it happened.

And as the last member of the jury filed out of the court, I gripped the edge of the dock hard and my heart was crying out to them:

"Please don't find me a killer. Please don't make a killer of me!"

HANK JANSON TITLES AVAILABLE FROM TELOS PUBLISHING

The true story
behind the
censorship and
banning of Hank
Janson's books in
the UK

2/-

THE
TRIALS OF
HANK JANSON

Steve Holland

The Trials Of Hank Janson

Steve Holland

In January 1954 twelve jurors sat at the Old Bailey to hear charges of obscenity against seven crime novels written by the immensely popular Hank Janson, whose sexy thrillers had sold five million copies in only six years. Hank's publisher and distributor were found guilty and imprisoned and an arrest warrant put out for author.

The Trials of Hank Janson presents a full biography of that author – in reality, a man named Stephen D Frances – from his early life, through the highs and lows he experienced with the Janson novels, to his eventual decline and death in Spain, cut off from the character he had created.

In addition, respected researcher and pulp fiction historian Steve Holland gives, for the first time, a comprehensive account of the early 1950s Home Office crackdown on so-called 'obscene' paperbacks – of which the Janson novels were the prime examples – during which some 350,000 books and magazines were destroyed on magistrates' instructions: a true story less notorious but no less remarkable than the controversy surrounding *Lady Chatterley's Lover*.

The Trials of Hank Janson also details the full publishing history of the Janson stories, from 1946 right up to the present day with Telos's reissue series.

'An intriguing history of a long-gone literary genre and the downfall of a bestselling author.' Sue Baker, *Publishing News* 'Highly Recommended'

344pp. A5 paperback original.

Illustrated with a 16pp full colour section of many original Hank Janson book jackets.

ISBN 1-903889-84-7 (pb)

£12.99 UK $17.95 US $24.95 CAN

SOME LOOK BETTER DEAD
Hank Janson

A seemingly innocuous visit to a fashion show leads *Chicago Chronicle*'s ace reporter Hank Janson into a web of murder and intrigue with dark secrets from the past.

112pp. A5 paperback reprint.
Includes an introduction by
pulp historian and writer Steve Holland

ISBN 1-903889-82-0 (pb) £9.99 UK $9.95 US $14.95 CAN

SKIRTS BRING ME SORROW
Hank Janson

Murder, blackmail, a femme fatale and switched identities ... just everyday problems for Hank Janson.

The Telos edition reinstates the previously-unpublished original cover artwork by Reginald Heade, which was censored when the novel first appeared in 1951.

144pp. A5 paperback reprint.
Includes an introduction by
pulp historian and writer Steve Holland

ISBN 1-903889-83-9 (pb) £9.99 UK $9.95 US $14.95 CAN

A Telos Classic

TORMENT
Hank Janson

Chicago Chronicle reporter Hank Janson is caught up in a convoluted web of intrigue involving telepathy, murder, grave robbing, pornographic photographs, infidelity and suicide! He is faced with having to uncover the links that bind all these disparate and seemingly unconnected events together and discover what really lies behind them.

Telos' publication of *Torment* marked the 50th anniversary of the book.

144pp. A5 paperback reprint.
Includes an introduction by
pulp historian and writer Steve Holland
ISBN 1-903889-80-4 (pb) £9.99 UK $9.95 US $14.95 CAN

WOMEN HATE TILL DEATH
Hank Janson

At a promotional event for a revolutionary new car, Hank Janson encounters cousins Doris and Marion Langham, whose wartime experiences in a Nazi concentration camp haunt them still. When a subsequent journalistic assignment leads Hank to investigate the gruesome shooting of Joe Sparman, who worked for the experimental car's manufacturer, he starts to suspect that the harrowing events of the past are having even more tangible consequences in the present ...

144pp. A5 paperback reprint.
Includes an introduction by
pulp historian and writer Steve Holland
ISBN 1-903889-81-2 (pb) £9.99 UK $9.95 US $14.95 CAN

WHEN DAMES GET TOUGH
Hank Janson

This anthology of ultra-rarities reprints the first three Hank Janson novellas – *When Dames Get Tough, Scarred Faces* and *Kitty Takes The Rap* – which initially appeared in 1946 over two volumes (with the latter two collected together under the *Scarred Faces* title). Literally only a handful of copies of the original editions now survive. Also included in this Telos anthology, as a bonus, are two Hank Janson short stories from the scarce *Underworld* magazine.

144pp approx. A5 paperback reprint.
Includes an introduction by
pulp historian and writer Steve Holland
ISBN 1-903889-85-5 (pb) £9.99 UK $9.95 US $14.95 CAN

The prices shown are correct at time of going to press. However, the publishers reserve the right to increase prices from those previously advertised without prior notice.

TELOS PUBLISHING
c/o Beech House,
Chapel Lane,
Moulton,
Cheshire,
CW9 8PQ,
England
Email: orders@telos.co.uk
Web: www.telos.co.uk

To order copies of any Telos books, please visit our website where there are full details of all titles and facilities for worldwide credit card online ordering, or send a cheque or postal order (UK only) for the appropriate amount (including postage and packing), together with details of the book(s) you require, plus your name and address to the above address. Overseas readers please send two international reply coupons for details of prices and postage rates.